THE DAY

SHE PRAYED

BY

PAT SIMMONS

@2023 Christian Reads Press/Pat Simmons

ISBN: 978-1-7338316-7-3

Developmental Editor: Chandra Sparks Splond
Proofread by Stuart Budgen
Final Proofreader: Darlene Simmons
Beta Readers: Evangelist Charlotte Townsend
Interior Design: Kimolisa/Fiverr.com
Cover Design: designerzone_lk/Fiverr.com

Praise for Pat Simmons

OMGreatness...5 Stars for Day Not Promised

My, my, my, my and MY!!! This book was so intense and emotional that I found myself interacting with the story as I read it. Pat Simmons' "Day Not Promise" had me praying, crying, speaking in tongues, lifting my hands, and rejoicing. You cannot read this novel without thinking about your salvation and those that The LORD has put in your pathways. –Reader Viv

Fighting Evil With The Power of Prayer and Sword of the Spirit...5 Stars for Day Not Promised

The urgency of facing our mortality and eternity in heaven or hell is carved into the lives of Omega Addams and Mitchell Franklin. Author Pat Simmons boldly and creatively paints clear pictures of what happens in the lives of those who choose to eat, drink and be merry without consideration for their souls. "Day Not Promised" is a gripping story anchored in Biblical precepts with shocking twists.

When Omega's and Mitchell's lives become intertwined after becoming victims during a gas station robbery, the stage is set for a furious battle between good and evil. I fell in love with Mrs. Helena, Omega's neighbor. Omega realizes her neighbor's friendly words of greetings to everyone hold spiritual intuition and power. Mrs. Helena is like a general in the army of the Lord. She is assigned to train Omega to recognize the enemy in the spiritual realm. The visualizations are so stirring, you must blink to ensure the images of angels and demons are still on the pages and not surrounding you.

As the first book in the Intercessors series, "Day Not Promised" whets one's appetite to know God more intimately. It also provokes us to consider our words when we refer to someone as a prayer warrior. Mrs. Helena prepares to pass her mantle to Omega. The fight for souls is real. The heartbreak when mothers, fathers, sisters, brothers, lovers, or co-workers reject salvation is real. Simmons pens a moving novel that makes a nice addition to any intercessor's arsenal. —Reader Robin Pendleton

THE DAY

SHE PRAYED

Prologue

But every man is tempted when he is drawn away of his own lust and enticed. When lust is conceived, it brings forth sin: and sin, when it is finished, brings forth death.—James 1:14–15

January

"You don't want to be a part of my wedding?" Omega Addams' hurt expression matched the heaviness in Tally Gilbert's heart as she declined the precious offer.

Wedding magazines and fabric samples were strewn across Omega's kitchen counter, while various bridal sites were open on two laptops.

Omega and Delta had been like bonus younger sisters since Tally had started dating their older brother, Randall. His name embodied love and respect. They would do anything for each other except... No, Tally wouldn't go down memory lane.

Her relationship with the sisters had changed when Tally broke up with Randall and broke his heart in the process.

She had her reasons.

Cheating—no.

Physical or mental abuse—no.

It was something more profound than that. Tally's soul was at stake. To save it, she had to cut ties with the fine, sexy, and lovable Randall Addams.

She covered Omega's hand with hers to soften the blow. "I will come and support you in any other way, being in the same wedding party as Randall would be too much tension." *And temptation*, she thought.

"Ha!" Delta, the younger of the two sisters, called out. Her dark, flawless skin reminded Tally of Randall's. "You mean sexual tension. When you two were together, the room would sizzle." Her lips curled into a mischievous grin.

Delta sounded like Tally's sister, Porsha, who had said the same thing. "Randall Addams is a temptation with a pop of steroids and an extra dose of testosterone."

But her relationship with Randall had been more than just hormones. Their love was potent, drugging, and addictive. Anyone could see it was genuine. They supported each other's dreams and put the other first. There was never any manipulation—ever.

"Fornication was one of many vices the Lord saved me from. God has made it clear that I can't love the world and the Lord at the same time. It's not fair to tempt Randall with what neither of us can have," Tally said.

"I understand." Omega mustered a smile. "You're still like a sister to us, but as your fellow sister in Christ, I think you're making the right decision. I know my brother is on your prayer list for salvation."

"Yep. In bold letters. Other names were added and scratched off when the Lord honored my petitions. Randall Addams hasn't budged."

Tally was grateful her friend understood. After all, the Lord had drawn Omega to Christ first, and Omega had witnessed to others after He had spared her life in a gas station robbery. At the time, Tally hadn't been a hard sell because Jesus was already working on her. Tally was ready to change, but she didn't know how.

When she left Omega's condo hours later, Tally's mind drifted to the night God had captured her complete attention.

It was a weekend, and they always spent the night together, either at her house or Randall's. They were doing everything married couples do without a piece of paper, and they were happy, despite the shame Tally brought on her parents by not setting a good example for Porsha.

"Respect yourself and your family. You're a jewel, Princess," her father had said.

"But I feel like a queen with Randall." She pleaded her case but couldn't win them over.

While she lay sleeping in Randall's bed that night, Tally woke up screaming and crying. Perspiration clung to her like hot flashes, and she blinked to look around the room. A plug-in night light flickered near the door. She panted, trying to fill her lungs with air.

Randall woke and asked what was wrong.

"I saw myself standing on earth, and it was on fire. Raging. There was no escape. I was about to be burned alive. I was so scared."

"It was just a dream," Randall had said. "I'm here, and I'm not going to let anything happen to you. He thought I had fallen asleep after he wrapped his arms around me and rocked me gently.

She would never forget that night. How could anyone go back to sleep after feeling the heat and seeing the flames? "I wanted to be saved from hell," she said aloud as she continued her drive home.

That had been the last night she slept with Randall. Confused, scared, and lost, Tally hadn't known what to do until Randall casually mentioned that his sister had "gone church extreme" on him.

Randall didn't hide his bewilderment with Omega. "Church is for hypocrites," he had said.

Tally wasn't sure that was true and didn't conceal her curiosity.

She couldn't wait to get Omega alone to hear more about her salvation experience. Omega had hesitated because Randall had threatened her not to bring up Jesus to his woman.

"Your brother thinks it's something he did and..." Tally had smiled. *"He's been trying to do little things to make me happy. He can't. I want a balanced life with the Lord."*

Omega had looked pleased and tortured at her announcement. "I don't think my brother is ready for a Jesus commitment."

Tally had sensed that by his disparaging comments.

"What are you going to do?" Omega had asked.

"I'm breaking up with him." Tears filled Tally's eyes as she uttered the truth.

That had been six months ago and counting, and her heart still ached for his hugs, but the Holy Ghost kept her from falling back into the lifestyle that God had warned her to escape.

Chapter One

*Now unto him, that is able to keep you from falling, and to present you faultless before the presence of his glory with exceeding joy, to the only wise God our Savior, be glory and majesty, dominion and power, both now and ever. Amen. —*Jude 1:24–25

August, Wedding Day

Tally finished her eye makeup, then finger-combed her hair that was growing out of its pixie cut style. Next, she scrutinized her appearance in a sleeveless orange dress. Finally, Tally admired the bronze polish from her pedicure as she slipped into sandals.

Why was it necessary to look good to her ex?

What message was she sending? "I'm doing good without you," or "I want us back together," or "See, I made the right choice?"

After taking a deep breath, Tally grabbed her keys and drove to her church. She was happy for Omega and Mitchell, whom many had dubbed the Holy Ghost power couple.

That's what Tally desired, a praying man who knew to call on the name of Jesus to slay demons. *Lord, whatever man You have for me, show me. Let him love You unconditionally, so he'll know how to love me.* Randall thought church folks were hypocrites, but hypocrites were everywhere.

On jobs.

In families.

Among friends.

Too much was at stake as the End of Time approached. Until Jesus returned as He promised, Tally stayed busy by volunteering at church functions, participating in the daily 5:30 a.m. call-in prayer line, and reading her Bible faithfully. She memorized Scriptures that the Lord dropped into her spirit to ease the sadness whenever she thought of the baby she had miscarried from the love she had shared with Randall.

Why was it so hard for her heart to let Randall go?

Tally sighed. She would come face-to-face with Randall Anthony Gilbert.

He was tall.

Built with dark brown skin.

Solid muscles of handsome perfection.

"Whew." It wasn't good to linger on what her eyes shouldn't behold to make her heart pant for more.

How often had Randall visited Christ For All Church within the year they had broken up? Twice—maybe—including today.

Randall's sister's nuptials had forced him to come to church. Tally chuckled, but she wasn't happy about his default visit. "Wouldn't it be something if God saved you right at that altar where you stood as a groomsman?"

Yeah. That would be perfect.

Wishful thinking.

Some things are impossible with man, but trust in Me, and all things are possible, God whispered through the light breeze that filtered through the crack in her window.

A funeral procession caught Tally's attention. A day of celebration for one family had delivered sorrow to another. She slowed down and let the cars, filled with mourners, pass. Tally mouthed, "God bless you," as she made eye contact with a woman in a passenger seat.

The lady nodded as if she'd read Tally's lips.

God whispered Romans 12:15, *Rejoice with them that do rejoice and weep with them that weep.*

For the rest of the drive, Tally prayed for the family's comfort and healing in the coming days. She wondered about the deceased. Were they ready for death? Did they want salvation?

Those thoughts occupied her until she entered Christ For All Church's packed parking lot. Her mood immediately changed at the sight of the happy wedding attendees—couples, little girls and boys, the elderly—some on canes—and countless others coming to witness a grand occasion.

Tally smiled and greeted familiar church members. Although she and Randall had dated for a couple of years, she hadn't met any of his extended relatives. The only giveaway of kinship was a resemblance. The Addams family had handsome and beautiful relatives.

Groomsmen were in position as she entered the foyer. She made eye contact with Mitchell Franklin. Although handsome without the evening attire, he wowed in his tuxedo. Omega would swoon for sure.

Mitchell grinned as Tally continued her way.

No need to search for Randall. She felt his eyes locked on her.

His presence was always overpowering. Tally denied the pull, in Jesus' name.

Stepping into the sanctuary, she scanned the left section, designated for the bride's family and friends, then Tally spotted her parents, Kent and Cynthia Gilbert, and her only sibling, Porsha.

"'Bout time you got here," Porsha whispered as the sisters exchanged air kisses. "I thought you might have changed your mind. I saw Randall. Smokin' hot." Her sister fanned her face. "I'm sure all the single sisters got their eyes locked on him."

The nonchalant smile was fake, but Tally squeezed her lips together anyway. Porsha didn't say it to make Tally jealous. She was giving her observation.

Tally's attraction to Randall wasn't based solely on looks. His caring personality and humor hooked her after the first date, so Randall's surrender to God's salvation remained a top priority on her prayer list. There was no indication that he would be removed from the list soon.

They would be equally yoked as a Holy Ghost power couple, too, as the Bible said—unless God had someone else in store for her.

Her mother reached over for a hug, then her father. Tally's breakup with Randall resulted in her parents submitting to the Lord's salvation.

"That was nothing but Jesus," her mom had said. Kent and Cynthia were amazed that anything or anyone could break up the lovebirds. Tally considered herself living her best life with Randall, but the Lord showed her otherwise. Her parents said it had to be no one but the Lord who could separate them.

The violinist started a soft chord as the groomsmen walked to the altar in full swagger behind Mitchell and Pastor Rodney.

It was hard not to stare at God's handiwork. Tally's mistake. She made eye contact with Randall.

His magnetic tug caused her to shiver, but the Holy Ghost gave her the strength to blink and look away.

Minutes later, Omega's bridesmaids made their entrance, which included her sister Delta. Plus, sisters Caylee and April—international models who had flown in to be a part of the nuptials. After Mitchell had protected Omega at a gas station holdup, Caylee and April testified how Omega saved their lives. It was a domino effect.

The flower girl was next, then the bride appeared on her father's arm. Omega—already pretty—was breathtaking. Happy. In love.

Tally glanced at Mitchell, and his expression softened. That warmed her heart. He loved her and outdid Randall when it came to protecting Omega. And that was saying something. Randall went overboard, safeguarding what he called his responsibility.

The music stopped, and anticipation grew as Pastor Rodney began the ceremony. "Dearly beloved, we are gathered here today in the sight of God and these witnesses…"

When it was time to exchange vows, Omega and Mitchell were overcome with emotion.

"Mitchell, I love you. You've been my companion, confidant, and prayer partner. Thank you for coming into my life and taking a bullet for me."

They chuckled. It wasn't a secret that Mitchell had body-slammed her to the ground to shield her from gunfire. That's when God showed them that angels were guarding them.

"Omega, I'll *always* protect your heart, body, and soul. I promise to love you until my last breath," the groom said.

The moment was tender and sweet as sniffs floated throughout the sanctuary. Tally chanced a glance at Randall, who wasn't looking at her. Good. *Whew*. She exhaled. But the longing on his face was unmistakable.

Then Randall turned and met her eyes. He didn't hide his hurt. Tally suffered the same ache, so she looked away. Her thoughts were jumbled.

Pastor Rodney pulled her back in. "By the power vested in me from the Lord Jesus Christ and the state of Missouri, I now pronounce you husband and wife in holy matrimony. Let no woman or man come between you as you honor your vows to God and each other," the pastor said before asking everyone to join in as he prayed for them. "Amen, Brother Franklin. You may now salute your bride."

Mitchell's movements seemed coordinated as he tugged her closer. He lifted her veil so nothing could hinder him from pressing his lips to Omega's for their first kiss as husband and wife.

"God, I want that," she whispered to herself but loud enough for Porsha to hear.

"Me too." Her sister sighed and slumped her shoulders against Tally.

They smiled as God whispered to Tally's spirit, *You'll be a bride one day. It isn't wishful thinking.*

I know, Lord. When You return in the rapture for Your bride, her spirit replied, referencing the ten virgins in Matthew 25:40.

The guests stood as the bride and groom glided down the aisle toward the exit, where they formed a receiving line to greet guests in the foyer. Paired off, the bridal party followed.

Brace for impact, her mind whispered as Randall neared her pew.

He slowed his steps as he approached with his bridesmaid on his arm.

"Praying for you, sis," Porsha mumbled.

Tally nodded and swallowed. *Yeah, I need it.*

Randall's eyes sparkled at her.

He still loved her.

She still loved him.

Why did that make her happy and sad at the same time?

Whatever he was about to say, his marching partner tugged him away.

"That was close, sis."

Tally glanced at Porsha. "Yep. Even after all these months, my feelings are still strong too. I'll congratulate Omega and Mitchell, then I'm out of here. My heart can't survive being in the same room with him."

"Want some company?" Since Tally wasn't staying for the reception, neither were Porsha and her parents.

Too bad for Porsha because her younger sister, who stood two inches taller than Tally without the four-inch heels on her feet, would be sure to garner attention at the reception. She had thick, shoulder-length hair styled to one side in curls and a baby face without dimples, which Tally had. Both always received compliments for their pretty eyes.

"Sorry. I'll need some quiet time after this." Tally knew her sister would understand, although she had never been in love.

Tally needed to give thanks for making it through today's temptation and renew her prayers for Randall to ditch his pride and repent.

Row by row, guests spilled into the aisle to form a line to greet the happy couple personally. Since Tally was on the end, she was the first person out of their pew.

The well-wishers hugged, laughed, and took selfies with the bride and groom, slowing down the line, which was okay with Tally.

Caylee squealed her delight when she saw Tally and squeezed her neck.

"I'll talk to you before I leave to return to Australia." She introduced Quinn, Mitchell's younger brother, with whom she was paired. He seemed infatuated with the model.

Tally spoke to more pairs until Caylee's younger sister, April, was next with her groomsman. Again, she received a warm welcome and a tight hug.

The young woman, now nineteen, was a polished professional who had surrendered to the Lord and was living her dream as a runway model overseas. Tally was aware that Randall was two couples away, and she guessed her ex was impatiently awaiting her arrival.

"Get it over with." Porsha nudged her. "You got this, sis."

Right. Tally swallowed the fear of yielding to lust and stepped forward.

"Hi. I'm Gina, Mitchell's cousin, and this is —"

"Randall," he and Tally said simultaneously as he scooped up her hand in an intimate handshake. She could feel her heart race.

"We were an intense couple at one time," he told Gina but never took his eyes off Tally. His caress sent tingles down her spine. "Hands still as soft as I remember." Randall boldly appraised her appearance. "You let your hair grow out. Beautiful."

Gina cleared her throat, making it obvious she didn't like the attention Tally received. Neither did Tally. She tried to inch closer to the bride and groom. Randall wasn't having it.

"We should have gotten married before my sister. It's never too late to kiss and make up. I'm willing if you are." His mesmerizing brown eyes challenged her as his nostrils flared.

Rebuke that spirit in My name, God's voice thundered.

"Every knee shall bow, and mouth confess that Jesus is Lord. The Lord Jesus rebukes you. Goodbye, Randall." Tally shook her hand free and congratulated the bride and groom with hugs and smiles without looking back at her ex.

She waved goodbye to her family and made her getaway to the parking lot. Her emotions fell apart in the car before she strapped in her seatbelt.

Chapter Two

But He gives more grace. Therefore, He says:
"God resists the proud, But gives grace to the humble. —James 4:6

R andall woke up Sunday morning with his mind on Tally Gilbert. He still loved her and missed her. How could the petite, shapely woman in heels be any prettier? And yet, she was more stunning.

Wow. Any other time, he would have swept her in his arms and devoured her lips in a kiss neither would soon forget, but Omega and Mitchell had already given him a verbal beat down that this day was about their love, not Randall's lost love.

Tally drained his strength, then had the nerve to dismiss him with a rebuke. They were never cruel to each other. Whenever they disagreed, no unkind words were spoken. Randall supported whatever goals she wanted to accomplish, and she had his back too. Tally was his heartbeat.

Her rebuke would have been amusing if she hadn't looked so serious. How could she not feel his heart pounding? At that moment, Randall was willing to compromise.

He could do church if that's what she wanted. "Not every Sunday. I have my limits." Randall couldn't guarantee every month. Football games ruled, and she knew that by the number of tailgating parties they had attended together and hosted.

"Nope. I'm not joining, converting, or praying more than I normally would." Resting on his pillows, Randall crossed his arms behind his head and stared at the ceiling fan.

Seeing Tally again kicked his senses into high gear. She was even more beautiful. He noticed her hairstyle was different, and her nails were trimmed and polished, not the elaborate designs she wore when they dated, which he'd insisted he pay for. But it was never about the money with her. She was happy just being with him.

Randall came to a decision. He would meet her on the church turf if she didn't come to him.

Think about what you're saying, man. Bells jingled in Randall's mind to alert him of pending danger.

He shoved off the warning. Randall wanted to see her again. The debate was whether he should make his presence in the church known.

Since his sister and Mitchell left this morning for their honeymoon and wouldn't be at church, Randall could go undercover. He didn't want to give the couple, or Tally, the wrong impression of why he was there. Randall climbed out of bed to put his plan in motion as he received a text.

Hey, bro. Did sparks fly with you and Tally at the wedding? LOL. Or did you meet some hotties? I want to hear all about it later, Logan Strickland texted. They had been best friends since college and fraternity brothers.

Logan was divorced with a four-year-old son. Since neither of them was in a relationship, they usually got together when Logan didn't have LJ on the weekends.

He and Tally had often double-dated with Logan and his former wife. Tally and Roxie were cordial, but they never formed a bond like Logan and Randall.

His best friend appeared more heartbroken over Randall's breakup than the dissolution of his own marriage. "You two just connected and were my role models," Logan had said.

Randall would talk to him later. Right now, he had a mission. "I'm goin' churching—two days in a row." He laughed and headed for the shower.

He arrived an hour later at Christ For All Church. Randall dropped his keys on the ground when he stepped out of his SUV. His shadow caught his attention. He guessed the dark figure on the ground was his shadow. As he studied it, Randall frowned. It appeared to be an odd shape, not a human form—not his outline. "You trippin' over something stupid. Should have gotten more sleep."

Shaking off the distraction, Randall refocused and began his confident stride, spying the ground as this shadow figure followed him like it was designed to do. It suddenly disappeared at the entrance of the church. The sun was still high in the sky. Where did it go?

Inside the foyer, an usher greeted him, but Randall declined her offer to find him a seat. He snagged a spot far in the back, hidden among the regulars as if he belonged but didn't. Once he made himself comfortable, Randall looked around for Tally and her family, who had followed their oldest daughter's path to God. Why didn't they resist as he had? Maybe then Tally would have accepted how ridiculous her conversion was.

There used to be a time when they could sense each other's presence across a room. He smiled, thinking about it. They were in tune with each other's emotions. Today, he hoped that wasn't the case. Randall wasn't ashamed to admit he was attempting to get his fill of her. The hand-holding, the bicycling, the cooking, and the simplest tasks like cleaning the kitchen were more enjoyable with her by his side.

Music serenaded him until Pastor Rodney, the same minister who performed the wedding, broke into his reverie. "Think about this: The Bible says in John 15:13: '*No greater love hath no man than this, that a man lay down his life for his friends.*'" He paused. "Would you lay down your life for a stranger?"

Randall chuckled. That's precisely how Omega and Mitchell met. Whenever he thought about what could have happened to his sister... Randall pushed back the thought of what-ifs. He would always have respect for his new brother-in-law.

Pastor Rodney continued his questioning. "For your country—aside from serving in the armed forces? I see a lot of nods. What about your enemy?"

A hush covered the sanctuary. Apparently, Randall wasn't the only fool.

"As crazy as that sounds, it's exactly what Jesus did. He died for mankind—all of us. The good, bad, and ugly. Your bad deeds and sins made us His enemy, but he nailed them to the cross. Was it worth it? Yes. What's the payback for the Lord's suffering?"

Folding his arms, Randall shifted in his seat. *Let's hear it.*

"Surrender," Pastor Rodney told his audience. "All the Lord Jesus wants from us is to appreciate His sacrifice and surrender our will in exchange for His will. Jeremiah 29:11 says, '*God knows the thoughts He has for us, and they are good...*'"

After thirty-something minutes, Randall had heard enough. He stood at the same time the pastor asked those who wanted Jesus to come to the altar. "I'm not the one," he mumbled and detoured to the exit.

Since salvation was free, there was no need for him to surrender.

In such a hurry to get out of there, Randall almost collided with another person without looking where he was going. His adrenaline was pumping through his heart as if someone were chasing him. He stepped out into the parking lot and shook away the uneasiness. He glanced down, and the shadow was back on the ground. Again, it had the oddest shape that denied the build Randall possessed. His mind was playing tricks as if it was a ghost or something.

"This is crazy." He kept walking until he slipped behind the wheel of his vehicle and exited onto the highway. His SUV wasn't a year old, and he still enjoyed the sleek interior and the smooth ride. Randall was about to activate his cruise control when a tiny voice spoke louder than the music that was playing.

Test the speed. How fast can you go?

Randall gave it some thought as he pushed the limit by ten…fifteen…twenty miles an hour. He wasn't the only motorist driving at a high rate of speed. Randall tried to keep up.

An incoming text to voice from Delta snapped him out of a trance. He immediately removed his foot from the gas. What was he thinking? Was he trying to kill himself? Had he zoned out?

"Hey, big brother. I overslept. Instead of meeting at noon for brunch, let's do one."

He exhaled as his heart continued to pound from the rush. "Sure," he replied as his voice converted to text.

This stunt wasn't worth mentioning to anyone—not his family, Tally, or Logan—that he attended church or this fast-and-furious stunt.

Minister Jude Martin had Sister Tally Gilbert on his radar for months. Time to make his move. He was drawn to women who put God first. A recent convert to Christ's salvation, Tally was faithful regarding church involvement, including prayer sessions—a must for Bible believers.

She was the perfect role model for converts who struggled with their newfound faith. He decided en route to Sunday school to make a personal introduction. Sister Tally had looked stunning at the Franklins' wedding. An olive green dress complemented her figure. He had planned to approach her at the reception, but she never showed up.

He had another plan to approach her after the benediction. He stepped out into the hall to take a call that was spam. He almost bumped into a man he thought he recognized as one of the groomsmen from yesterday's wedding. "Pardon me, brother." Jude was glad to see the visitor, but if his soul wasn't right with the Lord, he was going in the wrong direction. Another day wasn't promised for anyone to repent.

Before Jude could introduce himself, the man was out the door in a flash as if he were being chased by someone or something like the devil himself. Jude shook his head and would befriend him as a brother-in-Christ if he decided to visit again.

Back inside the sanctuary, he studied Tally as she and Porsha hugged their parents after the benediction, then the sisters lingered at their pew. Jude's stride was quick and precise.

"Praise the Lord, Gilbert sisters," he said as their parents spoke with other members.

The two had the same brilliant smile and hazel eyes, but that's where the similarities ended. The younger sister was a few inches taller and had a beige complexion. Tally's skin tone was medium brown. Her hair wasn't as long but framed her face and highlighted her dimpled smile. Gorgeous.

They returned his greeting in unison. "Praise the Lord, Minister Morgan."

"Sister Tally, do you have a minute?" He looked at her, then Porsha.

"Sure." She shrugged and leaned against the back of the pew.

Porsha didn't move. The lack of privacy wouldn't hinder Jude from accomplishing his intent.

"I know we casually know of each other, but I've watched you since you surrendered to the Lord last year. I wanted to invite you to brunch so we can get to know each other personally." Tally's sister listened, so he felt obligated to invite her too. "Sister Porsha, you are welcome to come along too." Jude held his breath as he waited for her answer.

Since he'd become a Christ For All Church member five years ago, God had elevated Jude with spiritual gifts. He strived to be worthy of the Lord calling him to minister. Other brothers in the congregation said he was a moving target because the sisters had their trackers on ministers who wore tailored suits, were employed, and didn't rely on a bus pass for a ride.

Jude stayed prayerful about which sister he approached to ask out. Most women blushed at his invitation.

Tally didn't.

Not a good sign when he wanted to win her over.

"Oh," Tally patted her chest, "Minister Morgan, I'm speechless and flattered, but I'm not available for a relationship right now."

Wow. Shoot the arrow and aim it at a brother's heart. A confident man, Jude knew he was walking in God's will, but he wasn't expecting her to decline his offer.

He smiled, displaying his thousands of dollars in dental work, then chuckled. "I don't work that fast. I'd like us to build a friendship as brother and sister in Christ. I met your sister and parents. No brothers...male admirers?" *Careful. Don't be pushy*, he coaxed himself.

"That's hard to answer, Minister Morgan."

Baby steps. Jude didn't force the issue. He was sure he wasn't the first brother in the church to approach her. "Please call me Jude."

"You're in a position where God placed you, and I respect that. I'm more comfortable calling you by your title."

Jude nodded. "Fair enough. I like your sincerity."

Tally and Porsha said their goodbyes and walked away, but he heard Porsha say, "Girl, that minister is super fine and seems sincere. You need to reconsider. At least pray about it."

Jude smirked. He had an ally. He'd put his interest out there. Now he had to nourish it from afar. He and Tally were meant to connect. He was sure of it. Now, God had to convince her of that.

"I don't want to date." Tally rolled her eyes. "I left a relationship to build one with the Lord. Seeing Randall again yesterday reminded me that I'm not ready to move on emotionally. That man has his name tattooed all across my heart."

"Okay." Porsha looped her arm through her sister's. "But when you're ready, Minister Morgan's still fine. Respectful. Built. A man of God. And the swag on that brother—wow. He can pray for me any time he wants."

Her younger sister could talk sass, but Porsha was far from a man-hunter. She was cautious too. Tally lifted a brow. "Then maybe you should have accepted."

"I said he could pray for me. Plus, he's attracted to you, not your younger sister. I'm waiting to follow your lead." She grinned.

Their parents had been concerned when Tally and Randall's relationship turned serious. Kent Gilbert was outraged that there was no ring or marriage certificate when they started to live together. It strained her relationship with her parents because Porsha usually followed in her big sister's footsteps. Praise God she hadn't in this instance.

Porsha didn't take men at face value, but Randall proved himself worthy as a big brother figure in Porsha's life. Tally loved him for that.

Randall silenced her parents' protests by how he treated Tally, catering to her every need, from gassing up her car to shoveling snow from her door to the car. He took her on shopping sprees just because. Besides watching sports and old movies, they loved to cook together. She connected with him. Randall made her feel beautiful by the way he looked at her. Tally's father was right. They had all the perks of marriage without the rings.

She exhaled. Randall had repeatedly justified himself whenever he pampered her, "Because you belong to me, and a man is supposed to take care of his woman before she asks."

Randall was so easy to love. He never ceased smiling whenever he looked at her and whispered his love. Why was he being so difficult about loving Jesus too?

Tally had never felt more cherished. They had discussed marriage, family, and children. Both their families were waiting for the official announcement that they were engaged at any moment.

The announcement never came because the Lord had called her to repent of her lifestyle. Not good that the thought of dating someone else flooded her mind with memories of Randall. Nope. She wasn't ready. Porsha nudged her, and Tally zapped out of it.

"Sis, if you want what Omega and Mitchell have, you have to keep an open mind."

Tally squinted. "I thought you were #TeamRandall." Why was she on the offensive? Her sister was trying to steer her away from temptation.

"I am, but I know your former boyfriend is stubborn and not one to back down. I don't want to see you hoping and waiting on a man who might never humble himself before God. I'm not saying Minister Morgan is a bad choice, but I don't think you should shut down your options."

"The words of wisdom from my baby sister. Noted." Tally exhaled.

"He's the first brother to ask you out since I've been coming to church here," Porsha said, "and that was the beginning of this year."

"That's because Mitchell played Father Hen over me, Omega, Caylee, and April before they left—calling us his crew. I guess with him off on his honeymoon, Minister Morgan felt brave and made his move."

"I've got a good feeling about him. If you decide to go out with him, I think he'll treat you right."

Would he treat her like Randall? That was the only benchmark she knew.

They hugged and parted ways at their cars.

Minutes after Tally changed and removed her makeup at home, she fell to her knees and seemed to pray like she never had before for Randall and his eternal life. The wedding had been too much too soon for her. Randall was right. That should have been them exchanging vows.

Tally cried so hard that she collapsed on the floor and felt too weak to get up, so she stayed there and whispered with a hoarse voice, "Jesus, you know all things. If Randall isn't going to get his act together, then help my heart to move on. In Jesus' name. Amen."

She closed her eyes, hoping today had been a dream.

Chapter Three

Put on the whole armor of God, that ye may be able to stand against the wiles of the devil. —Ephesians 6:11

Tuesday, Tally woke before her five a.m. alarm. The Lord's army prayer band started their one-hour daily morning prayer on a conference line at 5:30.

Tally grabbed her prayer list and stared at the names. Distant family, friends, strangers, and even some clients she had developed cordial relationships with at the radio station. Some names had a checkmark beside them—her parents, sister, a woman healed of cancer, a teenager who survived a drive-by, and a handful of others—when God had answered her prayers.

Progress was still needed on the person in the number two spot. Tally sighed. Judging from her interaction with Randall at the wedding, he wasn't close to surrendering.

She washed her face and brushed her teeth, then dialed the number and introduced herself when prompted.

"Morning, and praise the Lord, everyone. This is Sister Tally Gilbert."

A chorus of "Praise the Lord," "Hi," and "Good morning, sis," greeted her.

"Sister Gilbert, it's good to hear your voice. We missed you yesterday on the prayer line," Mother Kincaid, the prayer leader, said.

Guilty. She had binged on cozy mysteries Sunday afternoon and night. The result of her previous day's obsession was overdoing the snooze button Monday morning until it was no longer an option to stay in bed or she would be late for work. "Sorry. I overslept."

"That happens from time to time, but remember, stay faithful to God's business because Jesus is always faithful to us."

"Yes, Mother Kincaid." Tally liked the woman who had been good friends with Sister Helena who helped Omega navigate her new walk with Christ. When Sister Helena passed away, Mother Kincaid filled the gap to guide the "crew" through their salvation walk. The senior saint was kind and nurturing.

Others flooded the conference call, and at 5:30 a.m., Mother Kincaid asked if there were any prayer requests.

"Sister Nelson's son is in the hospital," one church member said.

"Pray for my husband. He needs a job," Sister Green started and rambled off other names and situations.

"Money is tight. I need a blessing," Brother Campbell added after he read his list. When it was time for Tally's prayer requests, nothing had changed from last week, "Randall Addams' salvation, protect the students and teachers..." She finished twenty-four petitions later. It seemed selfish to Tally to ask for her ex-boyfriend's salvation when others had more dire needs, but she believed in the power of prayer.

The group followed the Biblical protocol as Pastor Rodney instructed prayer warriors, "Thank Jesus first. Pray for others and their needs second, and let your own requests be last."

More than a dozen saints were praying. Tally had learned to listen as they prayed for God's will in heaven to supersede man's will on earth, rebuke demons' shenanigans, and for people to repent. She could feel God's presence as He fed them spiritual food.

An explosion of heavenly tongues filled the phone line. They were bold, foreign, and powerful; through them, Evangelist Conroy interpreted, "God is for us. Use your spiritual eyes to see God fight our battles."

An hour later, Mother Kincaid closed out the prayer with a Scripture. "Remember, when we pray, expect deliverance, salvation, and healing. Second Corinthians ten and four says, *'For the weapons of our warfare are not carnal, but mighty through God to the pulling down of strongholds.'* We destroyed yokes and barriers this morning. Have a good day, sisters and brothers. Remember to take Jesus with you because the forces of darkness are waiting to tag along wherever we go. Let's remain on high alert in the Lord, in Jesus' name. Amen."

"Amen" followed as the saints dropped out one by one. Before Tally got off her knees, God whispered to her spirit, *I will clothe you in godliness since your heart is to live holy for Me. Read Psalm 132:16. Trials are coming.*

Hours later, Tally arrived for the morning business meeting at KMJT, the St. Louis radio station affiliate of the Genesis Media Group. Overall revenue was down, but Tally's sales were steady. She had two leads to follow up on for new accounts and some cold calls planned for the day.

Her efforts had paid off not only in salary and bonuses. Yet, God had a hand in her promotion to senior account manager last year.

Genesis Media Group had been the highlight of her life. She'd met Randall during a cold call to his private IT company Tech Problems Solved. He ran an impressive firm. The attraction was there before she worked on the campaign, which bought him more prominent clients, a dinner, a date, and a love relationship that blossomed.

From that day forth, they acknowledged each milestone in their personal and professional lives with an intimate celebration just for them.

"This is a moment I want to share with you only," Randall had often said.

She missed him in her life, and seeing Randall again at the wedding after so many months apart confirmed it.

"Lord, I won't let the devil draw me back into that lifestyle." She meditated on Scriptures to fill her head to push forward instead of allowing the past to yank her backward.

After Tally left a cold call at a neighborhood bank, she stopped by the grocer for a few items. A young woman wheeling a shopping cart with a toddler strapped in caught her attention for no reason. An older boy and a younger girl were on either side of her. They were well-behaved and nicely clothed in denim shorts and T-shirts.

Tally admired the family image while God shouted, "Pray for her!"

Okay. Tossing her whimsical thoughts aside, Tally didn't ask questions or think twice. *Father, in the name of Jesus...supply her needs, protect her family, and encourage her soul, in Jesus' name. Amen.* Had she said enough?

She watched her from afar. The Scripture in Romans eight, verse twenty-six, came to mind:

The Spirit also helps us in our weaknesses. For we do not know what we should pray for as we ought, but the Spirit Himself makes intercession for us with groanings which cannot be uttered. Tally was relieved whenever the Holy Ghost spoke in heavenly tongues. Since God knew what the young family needed, the prayer would be on point.

What danger was God diverting from the woman? Was it a spiritual or physical battle? The Lord had given her friend, Omega Mitchell—now Omega Franklin—the gift to see visions, not Tally.

Help her, God whispered.

How? she asked the Lord. From what she could see, the woman wasn't in distress. *Lord, show me what you want me to see.*

God was silent.

Tally trailed the woman and children as her mind raced through possible demonic scenarios God was blocking. When it appeared that the little boy in the cart was about to climb out, Tally intervened. "Hey there. Be careful."

The mother apologized. "Thank you so much. This little one is my busybody."

"I'm glad I was here to help." Tally went on her way and exhaled.

Mission accomplished.

I guess.

Minutes later, the woman reappeared in the checkout line behind Tally. They exchanged smiles.

"I guess I'm following you," she said.

"Hi. My name is Carlton. This is my mom and sister—I call her Sissy—and my brother TJ." Her son rambled off the information as if Tally had asked.

"Hush." The mother squeezed her son's shoulder. "Sorry. If he knew my social security number, Carlton would have given that out too. I'm Sinclaire Oliver, and as you know, this trio belongs to me."

They were a nice-looking family. Tally guessed Carlton appeared to be about seven or eight years old. He was a lighter skin tone and slightly resembled his mother. *Must've taken his looks after his dad.*

Sissy and the toddler favored Sinclaire who might have been around Tally's age, give or take a year. The children were a perfect blend of cuteness.

"I'm Tally Gilbert. Nice to meet you. They are beautiful." She eyed the woman's cart. There were a few essential items to prepare a meal, but not one snack for the children.

How was that possible in a grocery store? When Tally and Porsha were small, a trip to the store equaled one treat apiece if they behaved.

The cashier totaled Tally's purchases as Sinclaire emptied her cart. That's when Carlton and Sissy asked for treats.

"We don't have money for that right now," she told the children softly.

Tally's heart broke, so she asked the clerk to add the chips and cookies to her bill that Sissy and Carlton had to put back begrudgingly.

Their mother looked embarrassed but reminded the children to say thank you as the cashier gave the children their treats.

After Tally paid for the purchases with a fifty-dollar bill, she tilted her head toward Sinclaire and whispered, "Give the mother the change."

Hoping she had done what God wanted her to, Tally left the store and added a silent prayer for the Oliver family. She wondered if Sinclaire was a single mother, divorcee, or separated.

As Tally was about to slide behind the wheel of her car, she heard a child yell, "Miss Gilbert!" It was Carlton, and he waved. "My mom says thank you."

"You're very welcome." Tally got in, touched her ignition button, and was about to drive off when Sinclaire hurried across the lot toward her with the children in tow. Her eyes were misty.

"Thank you," she stuttered in a whisper. "I really needed that money for gas, but I had to feed my babies." One tear fell, then another.

God, I know You honor humility. Bless this woman, please, according to Your riches in glory. Tally sniffed. "Do you mind if I pray for you?"

Sinclaire bit her bottom lip. She debated.

Why did people hesitate to receive prayer?

"O-okay," Sinclaire agreed.

Tally stepped out of her car and took one of Sinclaire's hands, and Carlton clutched hers. The small children held hands too. Tally prayed from the depth of her soul with authority in Jesus' name as Mother Kincaid had guided those on the morning prayer line. "Jesus, You're able to do abundantly, exceedingly more than we can ask or think when it comes to her needs." Heavenly tongues filled Tally's mouth as she conceded to the Lord. Tears streamed down her cheeks unchecked. "Whew," Tally said as she composed herself.

Carlton's eyes were wide in awe. "I like the way you prayed."

"Jesus wants all of us to pray to Him." She paused. "Sinclaire, I don't know what your needs are, but my church—"

Sinclaire's demeanor climbed from humility to the defensive. "I'm a single mother of three. Never married. I don't do church. Too much judgment. Too much drama."

"Life is drama, but God gives us strength to navigate through it. Hear me out. Christ For All Church is sponsoring our community day with back-to-school supplies, backpacks, a bounce house, games, gift cards...the works. Please come if you're not doing anything on Saturday from 10 a.m. to 3 p.m. I'll be there."

"Thanks, but no thanks." Sinclaire hurried her children away as if Tally had disrespected her.

Watching their retreat, she wondered how the woman could reject God after receiving a blessing from Him. "Lord, I don't think that turned out how You wanted." She had planted the seed. Let someone else water it. She got back into her car and drove away to another cold call not far from Randall's company.

———— *c&* ————

Early Saturday morning, Randall was about to stroll into Shade and Fade Barbershop in the Loop when an old longtime friend and fraternity brother walked out of a store next door and crossed his path.

"What's up, Randall?" Brian Duncan said and stuck out his hand for a shake. "How's that sister of yours enjoying married life?"

"Omega and Mitchell are happy. It's sickening," Randall half teased because their happiness reminded him of what he had with Tally. "How's your wife and the boys?"

"We are all good. When are you going to tie the knot with someone?" Brian asked.

Randall shrugged, then checked his watch. "No idea. When I do, we'll make sure to send you an invitation. Let me get in here and get my haircut."

"Sure thing. Good seeing you. Please tell your parents I said hello."

"I will."

Randall strolled inside as Cortez finished his client. The barber brushed fly-away hair from the chair and motioned for Randall to take a seat.

He had plans to meet his best friend, Logan, downtown in a few hours for the St. Louis Cardinals doubleheader against the Milwaukee Brewers.

Cortez and another barber ran a smooth operation on Saturdays with online appointments, so he wouldn't get backed up from walk-ins.

A man who seemed familiar stepped inside.

He must have recognized Randall, too, but Randall couldn't place him.

"I'm looking for Cortez. Don referred me."

"Jude Morgan, right?" Cortez asked.

Jude nodded.

"You're early. You can have a seat if you don't mind waiting fifteen to twenty minutes. This troublemaker here always wants the works," he joked about Randall who grinned.

Cortez pointed to a row of chairs. "Otherwise, you can run an errand and come back."

"I'll wait." Jude took his seat and stared at Randall. "Haven't we met before?"

Randall frowned. "Yeah. You look familiar, too, but I don't know where."

Jude shrugged and leaned back. He pulled out his phone, then paused. "Wait a minute. Weren't you at the Franklin wedding party?"

"Yep." Randall dared not bob his head and mess up Cortez's precision fade. "Omega is my sister."

"Right. Good to see you again. Are you planning on returning to Christ For All Church tomorrow? I saw you—"

Randall cut him off before he put his business out there. "I'm not church material."

"*Hmmm.* Interesting. I'm a minister, and I've never heard anyone say that before." Jude leaned back and crossed his ankle over his knee, exposing designer socks that complemented his color coordination. "What makes you think that?"

"My ex broke up with me because she's in church now and she says sex is off limits. People who call themselves Christians have sex all the time. What's the big deal?"

"Couples who indulge without the benefit of marriage aren't practicing Christians," Jude explained. "God calls His saints to live holy."

"Says the preacher." Randall huffed.

"Says the Bible," he corrected. "Sexual immorality between an unmarried male and female, two women, or two men is ungodly. Christ gives us His Spirit so we can refrain from sin's temptation and be rewarded in heaven."

"Man," Cortez said, angling Randall's head as the razor neared his ear, "you're overthinking this. Show up for church services if that will make her happy, end of story, and you'll be back in her good graces."

Randall was quiet as he considered his barber's advice. Jude didn't seem to have a comeback either. Was that the solution? He sure missed hearing Tally's voice and her giggles, and as gorgeous as she was, there had to be men inside those church walls ready to snatch her up. The thought made him furious.

"Yeah. It's not just going to church. Sex is important to me. I can't be with her without wanting to be intimate. That's an urge I don't want to quench. She doesn't drink anymore, not even wine. Jesus turned water into wine and partook. We're just doing what Jesus did."

"God created sex for husbands and wives to procreate. Men have twisted that. God created wine. Men have abused that with drunkenness. Shall I continue? Sin will make you think right is wrong, and wrong is right. Without holiness, no man shall see God. If you're struggling to live holy, God has the gift of the Holy Ghost to reign in the lusts of the flesh."

"Man, you sound like her. She wants to read, pray, and breathe Jesus. Not the woman I fell in love with. I want my old woman back, by any means necessary," Randall said as Cortez removed the cape from around him with a pop in the air, then brushed the stray hairs from his neck and shoulders.

"Come on, Mr. Morgan, I'm ready for ya," Cortez said as Randall opened his wallet and slipped out his bills.

"I'll be praying for you, brother," Jude said. "Seducing a saint of God has consequences. I wouldn't advise it."

Randall smirked and left. There wouldn't be any consequences if Tally Gilbert married him.

Chapter Four

Come unto me, all ye that labor and are heavy laden,
and I will give you rest. —Matthew 11:28

C hurch hurt was real. Sinclaire should know. She thought she'd met the love of her life at church. Carlton's father was charismatic and handsome. He seemed wholeheartedly interested in her.

Without a solid Christian foundation, Sinclaire thought he was a prize to snag. He wasn't a minister but might as well have been because they included him in everything. Since he convinced Sinclaire that they loved each other, sex was okay. They would marry anyway.

Wrong.

The ministers didn't try to counsel them to stay together when Sinclaire became pregnant. Instead, his minister buddies blamed her for tempting the brother. When Carlton was born seven years ago, the relationship between her and his father ended shortly after that.

Despite having children, loneliness crept in for years until Tyson Young Sr. entered her life. Feeling that he was a kindred spirit, Sinclaire had bared her soul as he professed to be a fixer of all her woes. He convinced her that Christians and non-Christians have sex as long as they didn't get caught. She had gotten caught pregnant again—twice.

Tyson's mother harped on them going to church and getting married. They did, and she felt uncomfortable by the stares and whispers. Every Sunday, the preacher's sermon seemed to be on her sins—sex, lust, and more. No one embraced her at that church, so before long, Sinclaire stopped torturing herself by going. That was breakup number two and enough of the dating scene for her to consider it a strikeout. Yep. Church hurt was real. Community event or not, Sinclaire wasn't stepping foot on any church property anymore.

The invitation wouldn't have come if she had enough money at checkout. It was embarrassing that a stranger had to step in and provide something so simple to her children that she could not. She tried to shop without them.

Sinclaire returned home and completed two freelance graphics and content writing projects before applying for another remote job. Without a full-time position with benefits, Sinclaire pieced together random contract work to meet the bare necessities. Whenever a top-pay project came along for her to save, one of the children needed something, or an unexpected expense like car repairs, new tires, or a forgotten bill came up.

If only she had a family to fall back on that would lessen the burden. Her parents were dead. She had no siblings. There were distant aunts whose first names she didn't even know.

No use dwelling on her situation. Sinclaire could use the help for school clothes and supplies but from church charity? *Nah. I'm good.* She had overheard two church mothers gossip after Sinclaire's pregnancy progressed with Carlton, "Well, she made her bed, so now she has to lay in it."

Memories from the past unsettled her, so Sinclaire dismissed them. "Get it together, girl." She exhaled and entered her kitchen and prepared spaghetti, salad, and garlic bread for dinner.

"Miss Gilbert was a nice lady, huh, Mom?" Carlton asked as he slurped on his spaghetti a half hour later.

"Mind your manners, young man," she softly scolded, then smiled. "Yes, she was."

"Mommy, can we watch a movie?"

How could she say no to Sissy's innocent eyes? "Sure, baby." Sinclaire reached over and wiped the girl's mouth.

"I'll share my treat Miss Gilbert bought me," Carlton offered. Despite having an imperfect absentee father, Carlton was the perfect son. Sinclaire smiled and rubbed his curly hair. "You're a good big brother."

After the kiddie movie, she listened as Carlton read to his younger siblings. Sinclaire was proud. Despite the bad decisions she had made, her children would do better. Carlton was selfless, friendly, bright, inquisitive, and polite.

Once the children were bathed and in bed, Sinclaire dreaded going to her room.

She feared sleep.

She feared darkness.

Stalling, Sinclaire checked her inbox for more work requests for digital artwork and content. When there weren't any, she sent her portfolio to more companies. A permanent job would eliminate the uncertainties of when more work would come.

It was late, and she was exhausted. Sinclaire craved sleep, but slumber wasn't her friend. Haunting visions about Carlton disappearing disturbed her peace.

They had reoccurred for almost a week now. It was eerie.

Although her eyes were closed, it was as if someone pried them open.

Carlton was at school. His classmates were taller and stronger than him.

They taunted him. "You're stupid and ugly."

Before her son could defend himself, his image faded from the classroom. The students and teacher didn't seem to notice.

What did the dream mean? She always woke in a sweat. It was too real. Every night, Sinclaire left her bed and padded across the floor of her two-bedroom apartment to the other bedroom where her three children slept.

Carlton, as well as her daughter and baby, rested peacefully.

Not being able to shake the frightful scene, Sinclaire never could return to sleep. The result was sluggish in the mornings.

"Lord, if you're listening, help me to sleep." She lay in bed and braced to be tormented.

Setting: the classroom.

Dark figures were coming for the children.

Suddenly, a bright light from nowhere seemed to circle Carlton like Plexiglas.

He was safe. It had never ended that way before.

Relieved, Sinclaire exhaled and drifted off to sleep. She woke the next morning refreshed. She grinned. God must have been listening.

The prayers of the righteous avails much. Tally prayed for you, God whispered.

Sinclaire's hands froze over her bathroom sink. Her facial cleanser soap began to sting her eyes. "Is that why?" She didn't know how she felt about God not listening to her, but Tally's prayers worked.

At the breakfast table, Carlton asked, "Mom, can we go to Miss Gilbert's church for community day? I want to be ready for school." His eyes were wide with hope.

"We don't have to go to a church to get school supplies and backpacks," she said, trying to appease him.

Carlton shrugged. "I think going to church would be cool."

Not cool. There were other places she could go for help.

Her day was slow without any new projects. She prepared lunch early, then walked the children to the neighborhood park to tire them out before it got too hot. That evening, she warmed up leftovers for dinner, watched a kiddie movie with her children, then prepared for bedtime.

Hoping for another restful sleep, Sinclaire climbed into bed. The nightmare returned. It was vibrant, and this time, she could hear voices.

"I'm bringing my daddy's gun," one boy said.

"I'll get knives from my kitchen," another said.

Sinclaire gasped. "Oh no, God. These children are planning a massacre. They're just babies."

It was as if they could hear her, and they stepped out of the dream and taunted her.

"We'll kill you too." The boys clawed at her, but Sinclaire fought them off.

"That was too real." She panted and surveyed her arms and hands for blood. On one hand, there was a fresh scratch. She must have been fighting in her sleep.

Instead of sweating, she shivered. She got up and grabbed her robe. Never could she remember having nightmares growing up. Last night was so real that her skin still tingled. She wanted to go to her children's bedroom and climb into their beds with them for safety as her two oldest often did whenever she had to bring TJ to her bed to quiet him down.

The next day, she tried to force the new images in her dream aside, but the vision haunted her now in daylight, following her from room to room and task to task.

She didn't have time for a distraction. Sinclaire had bills to pay. A month before school started was not a good time for assignments to slow down, but that seemed to be happening.

After waking up Saturday morning, exhausted from being terrorized, Carlton asked to go to community day.

"Mom, can we please go to Miss Gilbert's church?" he begged.

"Sure, son," Sinclaire consented. "Fix your sister and brother some cereal while I take a shower."

The weather for community day was hot, minus the humidity. Not the norm for August.

The news spread, and adults came with their children.

"God answers prayers," Tally whispered as she spied Sinclaire and her children through the crowd. Tally had added them to her prayer list and called out their names during the early morning prayer line calls.

Sinclaire made pit stops at stations for goodies and necessities for the children. She spotted Tally and headed her way at the same time as Minister Jude Morgan.

She was glad Sinclaire beat him and someone else had called his name. "Sinclaire, Carlton, Sissy, and TJ." Tally opened her arms to hug them like they were old friends, and they eagerly accepted her embrace. "I'm so glad you decided to come."

"Wow. A bounce house." Carlton pointed.

"Can we go, Mommy?" Sissy was two steps ahead, dragging her older brother.

"Yes. Play nice. I'm watching you," Sinclaire said as she switched hips to rest the toddler, who preferred his mother holding him rather than his stroller.

"We have something for TJ in the Tiny Tots Corner." Tally pointed to where her sister and two other church members played with the children three and under. Come on."

"He's two." Sinclaire kissed TJ's cheek.

There was no hint that Sinclaire had a problem with being at church, although they were outside in the parking lot.

Tally whispered her thanks to the Lord and waved at other guests she had invited. Finally, she and Sinclaire stood at the Tiny Tots area, cornered off for the younger children.

"This is my sister, Porsha. And this is Sinclaire and TJ." Tally made the introductions and the two women exchanged smiles.

"*Awww.*" Porsha's face glowed as she reached for TJ.

"I see the resemblance." Sinclaire smiled.

"Me too." Tally snickered while Porsha walked away with the child to where the small swings, slides, and colorful beach balls were set up for playtime.

"Since your hands are free, let's go to the eating area where there's shade. I'm so glad you changed your mind."

"I didn't plan to." Sinclaire had an unreadable expression while her children enjoyed themselves. "Carlton bugged me, so we are here because of him. For me, the church has been nothing less than drama—a place where I've been hurt, rejected and left emotionally for dead. That's my church hurt."

Sinclaire frowned. *"Hmmm.* That's not God's doing. It's people hurting each other. Jesus loves you, and practicing Christians strive to love each other. Otherwise, the Holy Ghost knows how to convict us."

"I don't think you're going to win this argument. I'm here because of my son. I do appreciate the freebies."

Tally grinned. "I don't try to win arguments. I try to win souls for Christ. I think we can become friends if you don't put up a wall. I'm sure your children can use another auntie."

The woman grinned and relaxed. "I don't have any sisters."

"Perfect. Can I give you something to think about?"

"Sure." Sinclaire sighed. "Go ahead."

"We get hurt at work, but we still show up every day; we get hurt by family, but we still love them; we get hurt in relationships…" Tally paused. Now she was preaching to herself.

"I get the point," Sinclaire said, not knowing Tally's thoughts.

Relationships. Tally hadn't gotten hurt, but Randall had, and she could do nothing to change that. Her eternal life was at stake.

The ladies approached the food table, where Mother Kincaid handed out smiles along with the snacks. She possessed a sweet spirit. "Praise the Lord, Sister Tally. Hello, dear." Her eyes sparkled when she greeted people.

In her eighties and a widow of a few years, Mother Kincaid was faithful in her church duties and loved to serve others. "Welcome to our annual community day. If there's something you need, let us know. We mean that. We are saved to serve."

An odd expression crossed Sinclaire's face before she gave a faint smile. "The tote bag they gave me is packed."

Mother Kincaid applauded. "Excellent. We're in the blessing business like our Father, the Lord Jesus Christ." She rested her hands on her wide hips. A big straw hat covered her face and hid her long gray hair tucked inside. She glanced around. "Looks like we have a great turnout. Pastor Rodney's about to give his hourly sermonette." She pointed to a white tent where rows of chairs were set up. Some had already gathered to escape the sun.

The microphone blared with a praise song that drew many.

Accepting their snacks, Tally led Sinclaire to the big tent as Carlton shouted to them from his post outside the bounce house, where Sissy played.

"Get your sister and come with us." Sinclaire waved at him. "I'll get TJ." As she retrieved her baby from Tiny Tots, he didn't seem happy to see his mother and leave the play area.

Tally waited for them so they could walk inside the tent together. Sinclaire seemed reluctant to accept the seat next to Tally. The woman was genuinely uncomfortable being there.

"Good afternoon," Pastor Rodney began after the song ended, "and welcome to our annual event. We want you to relax while your children play and enjoy themselves. First, here's a trinket to take home. In John 14:25, Jesus says, '*Peace I leave with you, My peace I give unto you: not as the world giveth, give I unto you. Let not your heart be troubled, neither let it be afraid.*' Whatever is troubling you today, God has peace. Whatever battle you think you need to fight, God can speak peace."

While her pastor spoke, Tally prayed for Sinclaire, hoping God would open her heart to receive whatever He had for her.

Pastor Rodney continued, "We have giveaways and gift cards for you today. Jesus has a gift for you, too, and it's eternal. Let Him be your strong tower where you can hide in Him. Does anybody here want to be safe and free from sin? Repent and accept the water and fire baptism in Jesus' name. Who wants that?"

"I do." Carlton lifted his hand as if he was in school.

Sinclaire frowned at him. Mother Kincaid, who had joined them in the row, nodded.

The more Sinclaire tried to talk her son out of the "nonsense," as she called it, the more adamant Carlton became. "God told me to come because He has something for us."

Mother Kincaid intervened. She reached for the toddler and snuggled him against her chest.

"You have a beautiful family and a smart young man. Salvation is not something to deny someone," she spoke softly, "especially children because the kingdom of heaven belongs to them because of their spiritual innocence."

"I have issues with the church," Sinclaire stated as her toddler clamored for his mother. Mother Kincaid relinquished her hold.

"As long as you don't charge God for other people's foolishness. Your son getting baptized does not mean he's a church member. He's joining the Body of Christ," Tally explained.

Sinclaire was quiet, then looked at Carlton, whose hands were folded in a pleading position.

Tally and Mother Kincaid held their breaths.

"Okay. I consent." Sinclaire looked defeated.

"Amen! One of the ministers will explain the reason for the baptism to Carlton and pray for him." Tally saw Minister Morgan and waved at him. He stopped what he was doing and met her halfway.

Tally beamed and made the introductions. "This is Carlton. He's seven and wants to be baptized in Jesus' name."

"You're a regular missionary for the Lord, Sister," he said.

"In a sense, I guess I am."

Mother Kincaid had said Tally was wearing a spiritual crown because she was winning souls for Christ. Within the past year, besides her parents and sister, she had witnessed to a sales clerk and a client. Both had surrendered to the Lord. Omega had a crown, too, because she had won souls for Christ, which included Tally.

"Just doing God's business."

"Amen." Minister Morgan stuck out his hand to shake Carlton's, then squatted eye-level with the child. "Tell me what you want from the Lord."

"I want to go to heaven."

The adults grinned, even Sinclaire.

"To do that, you have to repent—be sorry for your sins, doing things that you know have been wrong—to be baptized in Jesus."

"Okay." Carlton nodded. "Mom, are you going to repent too?"

Sinclaire jutted her chin in defiance. "Not today, son."

Not fazed, Carlton shrugged and followed Minster Morgan to the baptismal pool with three other candidates.

Tally didn't know Sinclaire's story, but she prayed the woman would repent one day and not be as stubborn as Randall.

Chapter Five

Casting down imaginations and every high thing that exalts itself
against the knowledge of God and bringing into captivity every thought
to the obedience of Christ. —2 Corinthians 10:5

Mother Kincaid greeted Tally at church Sunday morning. Her eyes were bright when she faced Tally's guest.

"Hi, Mother Kincaid." Carlton grinned wide as if under a light for a dental exam.

Although Sinclaire was not inspired to attend church, Tally had convinced her to let Carlton come.

And it hadn't been an easy conversation.

"I consented to my son's baptism, but I'm not committing to taking him to church every Sunday. That's where I draw the line."

"What if I take him?" Tally offered. "I'll pick up Carlton for church and bring him back after the service." Holding her breath, she prayed for a breakthrough.

It was silence on the phone until Carlton's mother huffed. "I guess that will be okay—for now."

Tally had to walk a fine line so that this woman wouldn't question her motives.

What happened that caused Sinclaire to shut God out of her life? Tally wondered.

Not only did Carlton have his sins washed away after he repented at community day, but bold heavenly tongues flowed from his mouth with spiritual power. God's anointing touched everyone near him, even Sinclaire, but the stronghold on Tally's new friend would not allow her to humble herself.

Stubborn. God reminded her of Romans 2:5 in the NIV: *But because of your stubbornness and your unrepentant heart, you are storing up wrath against yourself for the day of God's wrath when his righteous judgment will be revealed.*

Now, Tally had two tough souls to win over.

Carlton thrived on the attention he received from those who remembered him from community day.

Once they entered the sanctuary, Tally searched for her family to sit with them.

As the praise team led the worship songs, Carlton didn't need any prompting as he lifted his hands as if it was natural and closed his eyes. Tears streamed down his cheeks. Tally's eyes misted.

No wonder the kingdom of heaven was wide open for children. They were willing to accept the Lord's commandments. No questions asked. No rebellious spirit. Just pure innocence.

Pastor Rodney led a simple song as Carlton followed the words on the overhead screen. "The Jesus in me loves the Jesus in you…"

Tally was amazed at his hunger for God. Where some children played with a toy or watched a video on their parents' phones during service, Carlton was engaged in the worship.

Before the benediction, Pastor Rodney made the appeal for salvation. Two souls repented. They were baptized in water in Jesus' name and with the Holy Ghost.

Carlton leaned over and whispered, "I wish my mom were here."

"Me too." Tally prayed that she would be soon.

Afterward, Tally briefly chatted with Porsha. "I've got to get Carlton home. I'll call you later." She didn't want to create trust issues with Sinclaire about her son's well-being.

Minister Morgan appeared beside her as she walked across the parking lot. He had given Carlton a new Bible, and the boy carried it proudly against his chest.

"Brother Carlton, did you enjoy the message this morning?" He smiled.

Nodding, the child couldn't stand still. "Yes, Minister Morgan! And I can't wait to go home, pray, and come back again!" Carlton spoke fast as if he was going to run out of breath.

The adults exchanged chuckles, then Minister Morgan handed Tally a thick business card that seemed to be printed on premium stock paper.

"I know you aren't ready for me to get to know you, but if you change your mind, here are my numbers." He flipped it over. "This is my personal cell number."

Not wanting to come off as rude, Tally accepted it. She blinked at his job title.

An engineer at Boeing.

Handsome.

A godly man.

And…he was interested in her. She wasn't. What was holding her back?

At Tally's car, Minister Morgan opened her door. "Brother Carlton, take note. A young man should always open a lady's car door."

Carlton frowned. "Even my mom?"

"Especially your mom. She's a lady," Minister Morgan told him and chuckled.

Before Minister Morgan closed Tally's door, he said, "I'll be waiting for your call or text."

Right. She nodded. After double-checking their seatbelts, Tally drove off.

"I think you should call him Miss Gilbert," Carlton said matter-of-factly.

Amused by his input, Tally snickered and lifted a brow. "Really? You think so?"

"Yep." Carlton seemed nonchalant about his assessment, then glanced out the window to enjoy the ride.

Before dropping Carlton at home, Tally purchased a chicken family meal. Sinclaire was surprised as she hesitantly accepted food at her door. "Thank you. I...I wasn't expecting this." Sinclaire blinked back tears.

"Many of our blessings come when we least expect." Tally smiled and then drove home, processing what Minister Morgan and Carlton had said. She walked into her house. Quiet. No sound of laughter or children like at Sinclaire's.

She called Porsha. "Hey. I'm back home. Want to do a movie later?"

"Can't. I'm working on a presentation for work tomorrow. Sorry."

"No problem." Tally shrugged as if it were no big deal. Loneliness was real. She pouted. "Well, have fun."

"I won't." The sisters laughed and ended the call.

Who else could she call? Her parents were invited to a birthday dinner celebration. Tally had struck out. The weekends were the hardest for her when she always had something to do with Randall before her salvation. "But I'm living my best life with Jesus," she encouraged herself.

Going into her bedroom, Tally changed into comfy clothes and house slippers. When she removed her earrings, one fell on the floor. As she retrieved it under her dresser, the diamond tennis bracelet—a gift from Randall—caught her attention. She hadn't realized it was missing.

Memories brought a bittersweet smile to her lips. He'd given it to her when she'd semi-moved in with him. How was he faring?

Call him. It won't hurt to call and check on him. You two were friends before you were lovers, the tiny voice toyed with her emotions.

Tally had identified the devil's lure. "Jesus, You can keep me from falling and present me faultless," she said, quoting Jude 1:24.

You're bored. Friends go to the movies. Just don't sleep with him.

"I've been washed in the blood of Jesus. I rebuke you, Satan." Tally stood and stuffed the bracelet in the bottom of a drawer she seldom used. The more she fought back memories, the more they seemed to surface.

Grabbing her Bible, Tally took a deep breath. The next voice that came to her was Carlton's to call Jude. She shut that down. "I'm not ready."

Monday morning at 5:30, Tally was on the prayer line. She had moved Sinclaire to the top spot on her list. After Mother Kincaid closed out morning prayer, Tally called her to privately ask questions about Minister Morgan's character.

"He's a nice young man and is serious about the Lord."

That much Tally knew too. "But what about his social life? My sister, Porsha, thinks I should go out with him. What reputation does he have with the sisters around the church?"

"I think any mother or father would hope to have him as a son-in-law if..." Mother Kincaid was quiet.

"If what?"

"If he became serious about a sister in the church. I recall Minister Morgan seeing two other women in the congregation. I guess they were dating, but both sisters married someone else."

Tally squinted at the phone. "Don't you think that's odd? What's wrong with him? Do you think he's gay?"

"*Humph.* Hopefully, not on Christ For All's watch. If there is a hint of rumor or a revelation from the Lord about sexual immorality among leadership, whether it be fornication, adultery, homosexuality, porn, sex addictions—anything to do with the lust of the flesh, the pastor must take swift action and remove them from their post for a certain period until they repent and the Lord restores them. Jesus expects holiness from saints of God. Don't misunderstand me, the devil does come into God's sanctuary, but there's not room enough for the Lord and Satan. The Lord blesses a praying and fasting church because weeds try to choke out the grass."

Tally didn't interrupt as she considered her past indiscretions.

"Grab your Bible, and open to First Corinthian, the sixth chapter. Look at verses nine and ten: *"Know ye not that the unrighteous shall not inherit the kingdom of God? Be not deceived: neither fornicators, nor idolaters, nor adulterers, nor effeminate, nor abusers of themselves with mankind. Nor thieves, covetous, drunkards, revilers, or extortioners shall inherit the kingdom of God."* She paused. "But this next verse gives us hope that if we sin, God can restore us if we repent. *'And such were some of you: but ye are washed, but ye are sanctified, but ye are justified in the name of the Lord Jesus, and by the Spirit of our God.'"*

"Whew, I'm so glad that Jesus gives us grace." Tally gnawed on her lips. Good thing she hadn't started her makeup.

"Yes, but the day isn't promised, so we need to walk a holy life because First Corinthians ten and eight says, *'We must not indulge in sexual immorality as some of them did, and twenty-three thousand fell in a single day.'* All I'm saying, Sister Tally, is stay pure as you seek companionship within the church dating pool."

They ended the call.

Dating? Who said she was ready? An inquiry didn't mean…Wait a minute, she was protesting too much. If anyone knew what the Scriptures said about sin, Minister Jude Morgan should. If he approached Tally again for brunch, maybe, just maybe, she would set a date.

Chapter Six

Not forsaking the assembling of ourselves together, as the manner of some is, but exhorting one another: and so much the more, as ye see the day approaching. —Hebrews 10:25

The Lord had shown Jude in a vision that Sister Tally Gilbert was a woman after God's heart. Interested, he was determined to make his presence known in her life.

Unfortunately, Tally had turned him down twice. Last Sunday, he gave her his card. She never called.

Today, Pastor Rodney's morning message was encouraging from Psalm 37:23: *The Lord orders the steps of a good man: and He delights in his way.*

Jesus, You have always ordered my steps, so please touch Tally's heart, Jude prayed as he approached her following the benediction.

He was glad to see Carlton with Tally, but the child's mother was a no-show again.

Jude braced himself for Tally's polite brush-off as he approached her. Shocker. She didn't ignore him. "Praise the Lord, Gilbert family, and Brother Carlton."

After they returned his greeting, all eyes were on him and Tally. Jude didn't intimidate easily, but his knees weakened. "Sister Tally, have you given more thought to brunch, a movie, or a quiet park picnic?"

"I have and I'd like that." She lowered her lashes.

Huh? What did she say? Jude wasn't expecting that. He stuttered, "Are you sure?"

"Absolutely, but I have to drop Carlton off at home first."

"I'll make reservations at the Pancake House in Ladue. Meet you there in an hour?"

"Perfect. See you then."

Lord, that was too easy, but I ain't complaining, Jude thought as he escorted Tally and Carlton to her car as he had done before.

Carlton opened Tally's door as Jude had instructed last week. "Well done, young man." He shook Carlton's hand, and the child beamed.

In his car, Jude made reservations on his phone. The wait was forty-five minutes. He didn't see Tally's car when he arrived at the restaurant. Jude went inside to double-check his reservation, then stepped outside to watch out for her. She appeared minutes later. Instead of being alone, Carlton was still with her.

What happened?

Jude met her halfway in the parking lot. "Is everything okay? I thought you were taking Brother Carlton home."

"Me too—or rather, I did. Sinclaire wasn't there. She was out with the other children at the Magic House and lost track of time. She said I could wait in my car with Carlton, or if I didn't mind, drive him out to Kirkwood to the Magic House." She paused and seemed hesitant to continue. "I came up with a Plan C—bring Carlton with me, otherwise I would have been late, and I didn't want you to think I stood you up."

Thoughtful. Jude liked that.

"I hope you don't mind?" she asked with an uncertain expression that matched Carlton's.

"Of course not." They both looked relieved. "I'm sure they can add a plus-one to our reservation."

"Thank you, Minister Morgan." The boy grinned, clutching his Bible under his arm instead of leaving it in the car.

Jude felt this baby saint would grow into a man of great faith if he diligently read the Word of God.

Once the trio was seated in the booth, Jude sat across the table from them. Their server appeared with the menus and placed three glasses of water on their table.

"Brother Carlton, what do you have a taste for?" Jude asked. Even though he hadn't planned for a third wheel, it was important not to leave him out of the conversation.

"Can I have waffles with a lot of whipped cream?" Carlton asked, straightening his body to wait for the verdict.

"Of course, you may. How about a glass of milk to go with it?" Jude had no idea why he said that as if he was a parent. The thought amused him.

Carlton nodded. "Milk is okay."

"Sister Tally?" Jude watched her as she scanned the menu, then rested it on the table and smiled at Carlton.

"I'll have what my friend is having."

"Yes!" Carlton grinned. He looked so proud.

"I'll take the triple meat omelet," he said, handing over his menu to the hostess. Jude put on hold the conversation he had planned to get to know Tally. Since Carlton was with them, he wanted the boy to feel welcomed.

"What grade are you in, and what's your favorite subject?" he asked safe questions that didn't include his father's whereabouts.

"I'm going to the second grade. Mrs. Parks is going to be my teacher…"

Tally listened along with Jude as Carlton rambled on about things that were important to him.

Carlton paused when their food arrived.

They thanked the hostess, then Jude reached across the table for their hands to pray. Tally's fingers were soft and dainty. He was gentle in his grip.

"Lord, in the name of Jesus, thank You for this friendship with Tally and Carlton. Please bless and sanctify our food, removing anything that can harm us, and remind us always to feed those who are hungry in Jesus' name."

All three said, "Amen."

"I'm going to pray like you one day, Minister Morgan, and I'm going to share my lunch at school if anybody is hungry too."

An indescribable emotion swelled up in Jude. Carlton was easy to nurture, causing Jude to crave a son of his own. "Amen. I believe God will use you for great things." Then he cut into his omelet.

While Tally was quiet throughout their meal, Carlton was full of questions. "Do you have a girlfriend?"

Tally blushed.

Lord, this may get interesting. Jude chuckled. *Thank You for sending this young man to break the ice between me and Sister Tally.* "I'm working on it."

Carlton grinned. "Good, because I like Miss Tally."

"That makes two of us." Jude glanced at her, then held up his fist for Carlton to bump it.

"Excuse me, you two, but I'm sitting right here." Tally squinted at both of them.

"We know," he and Carlton said in chorus. "Okay, I don't want you to feel uncomfortable."

They ate in silence until Tally asked why it was hard for some people to come to Christ after witnessing to them. "Don't get discouraged. Unfortunately, everyone doesn't repent right away, if at all. Their salvation could be delayed for years."

"I hope not." Tally groaned.

"Me too. I want Jesus to save my mommy and my baby brother and Sissy." Tilting his head, Carlton twisted his lips in thought. "My dad too."

"Good. We have to be in this spiritual fight for souls for the long haul. One of the church mothers had testified that God had saved her brother forty years after he saved her. That's a guaranteed spot in heaven."

Tally nodded, then took another bite of her waffle. "I want to think I'm on a roll witnessing.

"You're on fire for sure." Jude grinned and forked off another bite of his omelet. *My kind of woman.*

They lost track of time as patrons left and others came, until Tally's phone rang. It was Sinclaire. Tally nodded and ended the call.

She faced Carlton. "Your mom's at home, so it's time for us to go."

Carlton slumped his shoulders, and his disappointment matched Minister Morgan's. The Lord had shown him Tally as a sister in Christ he should get to know. Jesus hadn't prepared him for the sudden craving for a family as he requested the bill, then walked them out to the car.

"This was fun. Thank you for treating us to brunch," Tally said as Carlton beat Jude to opening her door.

"I hope there will be a next time." Jude hoped for Tally's confirmation.

"Me too, Minister Morgan," Carlton said.

Jude snickered. "Sister Tally, you have made my day. I hope we can fellowship again soon. A movie, picnic, bicycle ride…whenever you don't want to be alone, call me."

"I will," she said.

When she drove away, Jude slipped his hands into his pants pockets, wondering if she would.

Chapter Seven

Though he slay me, I will still trust Him:
but I will maintain my ways before him. —Job 13:15

Tally was excited to attend her first all-night prayer shut-in. Mother Kincaid reminded those on the morning prayer line that spiritual warfare was real on this earth and people must be in a spiritual state to slay the demons.

Thank God Friday was her light workday. After she met with two clients, she planned to go home and rest. Tally was on a mission to free the captives that the devil had in a snare… friends, family, and strangers. The harvest was ripe for the pickin'.

Go see Sinclaire, God whispered.

O-okay. Tally sighed. There went her power nap, she thought as she called Sinclaire. "Thinking about you. Is it okay if I stop by?"

"Sure." TJ cried in the background.

When Tally arrived a short time later, her spirit suddenly felt anxious when she entered the apartment. She saw nothing that seemed unusual, but Tally felt dark spirits were tuckered away out of sight, ready to torment. What was going on?

She had a lot to pray for.

Sinclaire seemed flustered with the two-year-old as Sissy vied for her mother's attention. Where was Carlton in the middle of this chaos?

He appeared seconds later, walking out of the bathroom, and seemed unfazed by the racket. "Hi, Miss Tally. Praise the Lord." He beamed with the church greeting. "Guess what I read in my Bible?"

"Not now, son. Not now." Sinclaire's voice held an edge as she rubbed her temple.

"What's wrong?" Tally asked.

"Just tired. I'm not sleeping well at night," Sinclaire said. The dark circles under her eyes against her fair skin showed the evidence.

"Are you sick? Is it something you're eating before bed?" She took a seat, and TJ climbed on her lap. Sissy sat next to her. Is this what motherhood would be like for Tally if she had not lost her baby?

"No...Carlton, take your brother and sister into the bedroom and play while I talk to Miss Tally."

Her son obeyed without question.

"I keep having nightmares," Sinclaire said in a low voice once they were alone. "Plus, I'm worried about my finances."

"Are you getting child support?" Tally felt that was the obvious question.

"*Ha.* From which deadbeat father? There are two. Carlton has a different father from my daughter and her baby brother."

"Oh."

Don't judge. This could be you as a single mother, God reminded her.

Tally wanted to argue that Randall would never let their child do without, but God knew Randall better, and maybe the Lord was talking about Tally in another relationship.

"Sinclaire, those men are their fathers. They need to help. If they don't do it on their own, force them." Tally tempered her words so as not to come off as scolding. "I can see that keeping you up at night."

"Yeah, and…" She paused. "I feel like demons are around here. It's tormenting, but when I hear my son pray, a calmness fills this place. Sometimes I wish I could pray like Carlton."

God gave her an open door to witness for Him. "You can. It starts with one word that became flesh—Jesus."

"I told you I'm not ready for the church thing." Sinclaire gave Tally the side-eye.

Why was she fighting against something she clearly saw the benefit of having? Tally kept her thoughts to herself.

"I'm going to our prayer service tonight. Hundreds of us will lay our requests before Jesus all night. I'll pray for God to give you the courage to make some life changes about financial assistance from the children's fathers."

Sinclaire shivered and grunted out a chuckle. "I wonder if I can get some sleep there."

"Where?" Tally frowned.

"Never mind." Sinclaire shook her head and snickered, but nothing was funny. "I don't want to go to court. I'd rather show both losers that I don't need them. I can take care of my children."

Tally held her mouth until she could find the right words. She exhaled. "But you're struggling, Sinclaire. You may not need their help, but your children could use it." Tally stood. "Do you mind if I pray before I leave? The Bible says at the name of Jesus, demons tremble."

Carlton burst out of his room with his sister and brother trailing. "Yeah, let's make them scared."

Sinclaire squinted. "Boy, were you eavesdropping? I told you about that," she scolded.

"Sorry, Mom. Can I lead the prayer?" Carlton asked, and Sinclaire nodded.

"Jesus!" he cried out like thunder, and the room seemed to rumble with force. He prayed, then prayed some more until he wore himself out.

Whether Sinclaire realized it or not, she was in the good hands of a young prayer warrior. Tally continued the prayer, "Jesus, please provide for Sinclaire's family, give them peace and protection. You are faithful, even when we are not…"

After Tally lifted the final Amen to the Lord, a calmness descended, and peace engulfed the atmosphere.

Sinclaire sniffed, walked Tally to the door, and spoke quietly. "Thank you, and I'll think about what you said. I get something for Sissy and TJ, but it's inconsistent."

"It sounds like a bribe to keep you quiet, but your babies deserve more. Be prayerful. Do it for your children, especially Carlton."

Sinclaire rolled her eyes. "His dad changed jobs last I heard, so I don't know where he is now."

"God knows, and the law can track him down. I've got to go now. Love you all." Tally gave and received hugs.

"I wish I was going." Carlton came to his mother's side with a sad expression.

"Son, you're knocked out when your head hits the pillow."

"Maybe one day." Tally said her goodbyes and hurried home.

Hours later, Tally arrived at church at the same time as Mitchell and Omega—the newlyweds were parking. Tally tapped her horn and snagged a spot not far away. They waited for her as they were holding hands. They were all smiles.

"Hey, you two." Tally grinned. She hugged Omega first, then Mitchell. Both were dressed in light-colored denim. Mitchell had on a short-sleeved shirt with his jeans; Omega wore a denim jumper.

As long as she had known Omega, Tally had never seen her glowing. "What are you two doing here?"

"*Duhhh*. It's a shut-in," Mitchell said with a snicker.

"I know that, but aren't you two still supposed to be on a honeymoon—"

"What better way to start our marriage but in prayer? A family that prays together stays together." Mitchell tugged on Omega's hand.

Falling in step with the couple, the trio strolled toward the entrance with other prayer warriors.

About a hundred members were inside the sanctuary. Porsha was there, too, with a throw pillow cuddled to her chest. Quietness filled the atmosphere—a reverence for God—so her sister waved.

Tally separated herself from Omega and Mitchell and headed toward the middle section of the sanctuary. She spied Mother Kincaid about to bend her knees with a throw pillow for a cushion against the hard carpeted floor.

Pastor Rodney tapped the mic. "Praise the Lord, warriors. It's almost nine, so let's consecrate our minds to go boldly before the throne of God. This is serious business. People have asked us to pray for them. Let's do it."

"Yeah," many shouted, clapping.

"Amen. We will pray until seven in the morning. If you don't think you can endure, the brothers will escort you to your cars at midnight. Otherwise, we're in this together. Ministers will walk through the sanctuary praying to keep everyone on one accord so you won't doze off. We want to receive victory over our petitions tonight." With that said, he lifted his tambourine and began to sing, "I'm a Soldier in the Army of the Lord."

Everyone joined in until voices of praise turned into voices of prayer as the saints cried out to the Lord.

Resting on her knees, Tally closed her eyes and cried her heart out to the Lord, beginning with those on her prayer list. She started with Sinclaire. *Jesus, You know what she needs. I bind the demons in the name of Jesus. Break the yoke of fear....* She sighed when she got to Randall's name. *"Lord, Your promise is true. Whatever is hindering him, I rebuke those spirits that are strangling him....*

Hours later, when she ran out of energy, Tally heard one of the ministers nearby worshipping and praising God. "Bless those who bless us and have mercy on those who hurt us..."

Tally didn't know what prompted her to open her eyes, but when she did, Tally squinted. Angels paraded up and down the aisles as if creating a force field that no one could penetrate.

Tally prayed harder until she heard the bell ring.

"It's midnight, saints. If you need to leave, the ministers will walk you to your cars," Pastor Rodney said, then continued his prayers.

Coming from nearby, Porsha said, "That's my cue, sis. Good night."

"Be careful going home," Tally whispered, then resumed praying. She wasn't going anywhere. Tally had a lot to pray for. *God, let me see salvation...salvation...salvation...*

Throughout the night, whenever the voices seemed to quiet, a wave of prayers or praise engulfed everyone and energized them to keep praying.

She hadn't realized she had dozed until someone tapped her shoulder. Tally stirred and blinked. She looked up and around. No one was there. Not even close by.

At seven in the morning, Tally stood, yawned, and stretched. Her body was exhausted and hungry, but her spirit was on fire, joyful that God heard their prayers. She glanced across the sanctuary. A good number of members had remained after midnight. She saw Mitchell stand and walk to the other end of the pew where Omega had been praying and helped her stand, then the two hugged.

Tally smiled. She desired to be part of a Holy Ghost power couple. Her longing intensified as she watched them.

Minister Morgan came sluggishly to her side and stretched. "Nothing like being on a spiritual battlefield for the Lord, huh? This isn't your first time in shut-in prayer service."

"No, it's not. I may have dozed a few times," she said as her mind was still on the newlyweds. *A family that prays together stays together*, Mitchell had said. No wonder the Scripture said not to be unequally unyoked. *I want a praying husband.*

He studied her until she became uncomfortable. "What?"

"You got some serious backup, sis." Minister Morgan continued to stare, so Tally frowned. "What I mean is angels surrounded you while you prayed."

"That's good to know." Excitement filled Tally. If she had the energy, she would have done a victory dance. Spiritual warfare was real. Saints needed to win on the battlefield. She limited her conversation with him because of her morning breath.

She spied Mitchell leaving the sanctuary with his arm around Omega's waist. Others, including she and Minister Morgan, exited the church overhearing conversations about whether to eat or go home to sleep.

It was a toss-up for Tally when Minister Morgan offered to treat her to breakfast.

"It's just the two of us today." His smile was genuine despite the weariness in his eyes.

Sleep sounds so much better to me. She graciously declined his invitation, stifling a yawn.

Tired but spiritually refreshed, Tally got into her car and couldn't wait to get to bed. She expected the traffic to be light early on a Saturday morning.

She slowed down as she passed a strip mall. Three Black men were throwing bricks into a store's display windows. They were trying to break in.

Shocked to see a crime in progress rather than a replay on television, Tally's first mind was to interrupt them.

Pull over to the side, God spoke.

Tally's heart raced as she did. Now what? She was a sitting target.

Lower your window and whisper, "Jesus is coming."

A whisper? She wanted to question God but did as He instructed.

"Jesus is coming," she said softly. What came out of her mouth was the roar of a lion. She blinked at the sound of an army approaching on horseback. She couldn't tell from what direction.

Whatever the men saw, Tally wasn't privy to. The presence of the Lord had caused the men to drop their makeshift weapons and jump into two cars. Before they could flee from the parking lot, two patrol cars with sirens blaring blocked them in.

"Wow." Tally closed her jaw and continued home. "I'm a witness, prayer works."

Chapter Eight

Therefore, take no thought, saying, What shall we eat? or, What shall we drink? or, Wherewithal shall we be clothed? (For after all these things do the Gentiles seek) for your heavenly Father knows that ye have need of all these things. —Matthew 6:31–32

S unday's service at church was on fire as the saints testified about healings and deliverance after the all-night prayer service. The baptisms on Sunday were nonstop.

"Truly, we have the victory," the pastor said.

After the benediction, Tally and Porsha left in high spirits. She shared with her sister what happened on the way home after the shut-in.

"What? Girl, you were brave." Porsha's jaw dropped in disbelief. "I'm glad you weren't hurt."

"Me too. Maybe that's why Minister Morgan said he saw angels surrounding me at the shut-in."

Porsha's lips curled into a smile. "He likes you, but I heard you praying for Randall when I came to tell you I was leaving."

"I always will." Tally nodded. "When I saw Mitchell and Omega praying at opposite ends of the pew, I got a glimpse of what it looks like to have a praying husband."

"Speaking of glimpse, Minister Morgan just spotted us, and he's coming our way. Does he have a chance with your heart, or does Randall still have it hostage after—what—it's coming up on a year, right?"

"Yep, but I don't know if any man has a chance." Tally sighed, shaking her head. "Minister Morgan and I went to brunch last week—"

"What? And you didn't tell me." Porsha lifted her brow.

"With Carlton as our buffer. I like Minister Morgan and respect his position, but I don't want him to think we have a routine, you know? I'm learning that healing from a broken heart is a long process. God will help me move on."

"Praise the Lord, Minister Morgan." Porsha smiled.

Tally glanced over her shoulder. The brother was packaged with handsomeness, but there wasn't an instant connection.

"Praise the Lord, sisters." His eyes sparkled when he faced Tally. "Have you regained your strength?"

"Somewhat."

"How about lunch or brunch?" he asked.

Tally tried to find the right words. "Do you mind if I get back to you? I'm trying not to lead you on. When I said I wasn't ready for a relationship, I meant it. Plus, I have to drive Carlton home." She scanned the sanctuary and saw him playing with other children his age.

Minister Morgan seemed either annoyed or offended. Tally couldn't tell when he said, "I thought we were building a friendship. Carlton is welcome to join us at any time."

When someone called his name, Minister Morgan excused himself and didn't look back.

"Whew, girl. How can you resist that confidence? Don't play with him." Porsha gritted her teeth as if she were being tortured and pointed at his swagger.

Chuckling at her sister's antics, Tally shook her head. "It's not hard for me to resist."

"What if Randall never surrenders?" Porsha folded her arms.

Tally didn't want to entertain that as a possibility. "I love Randall, and if I called him today, we would be back as a couple—an unequally yoked one that God would disapprove of.

With Randall comes temptation, and I care about his soul. I hope and pray that one day, he will repent of his sins and be baptized in Jesus' name, not for me, but for himself. Now, can we talk about something else besides a man?" she said as Carlton joined them with his new friend.

After Carlton introduced Jalen, Tally said it was time for them to leave so she could take him home.

"Are we going to eat with Minister Morgan again?" His face was bright with anticipation.

Not him too. Tally withheld her groan and offered a smile. "Not today." Tally hugged her sister goodbye who gave a smug smile.

She wasn't ready for a relationship. She wasn't ready for a relationship. She wasn't ready...Tally repeated quietly as she and Carlton walked to her car without further mention of Minister Morgan.

He wasn't the one.

At mid-week Bible class, Minister Morgan waved to Tally and Porsha but kept his distance.

Grateful for the space, Tally exhaled.

With the upcoming three-day Labor Day weekend, she was in work mode and planned to finish her sales strong for the month with two pending new accounts.

What she didn't expect was a life-changing decision from the station manager, a no-nonsense, younger than her tanned White man who was quick to say no without a blink of an eye and yes without a pat on the back for a job well done.

"You've done a great job, Tally, but we can't afford to keep you on. We have to cut our budget, and your salary is mid-level. I'll give you letters of reference, and of course, you have severance pay."

It was a done deal within minutes. No questions could be asked or negotiations possible as Mr. Gray—Gary Gray—dismissed her from his office and asked her to send in another colleague who was probably next on the list.

Never let them see you sweat.

"Thank you for allowing me the opportunity. I'll go pack up my things."

Tally walked to her cubicle, fighting back the tears. Once at her desk, she turned her back to onlookers so she could process her new reality. Unemployed? She was living a victorious life. How could this happen? Why didn't God give her a heads-up?

She loved her job of ten years. Now what? Questions swarmed in her head. Tally had a condo note, car payments, student loans...

Peace! God thundered. *Trust in Me. Your trials come to build up your faith.*

I do trust You, Jesus. I'm mad that the devil is retaliating after the all-night prayer shut-in service. Standing, Tally swallowed back the fear of the unknown. She would break down in private.

She packed her boxes quickly. Ten years worth of awards, gifts from clients...memories. She packed what she could with the empty boxes at hand so she could get out of there.

Less than an hour later, Tally smiled at the staff who knew her fate as she walked out.

Once in her car, her tears flowed. She tapped Porsha's number and got her voicemail.

"Great. When I really need to talk to someone." She felt alone. Had God forgotten about her?

Call Minister Morgan.

Was that her mind talking to her or God? she questioned.

Resting her forehead on the steering wheel, Tally closed her eyes. What a difference a week made. Last Friday, she was gearing up, preparing for a spiritual battle. This Friday, she'd suffered a defeat.

She riffled through her purse for a tissue. Minister Morgan's card fell out. She squinted to read it through blurred vision.

First, she had to stop crying, which could take a while. Tally started her car, so the air conditioning's coolness could brush up against her swollen eyes. She took a deep breath and was able to steady her breathing.

She called his number. When he answered, tears exploded from within her. "Ah, Minister Morgan, this is…"

"Sister Gilbert, what's wrong? Talk to me."

He didn't know she was trying, but all the working parts to form a coherent conversation weren't aligned.

Minister Morgan was patient as he softly began to pray. "Lord, be with her. Strengthen her faith in whatever she's going through. Let her know You'll never leave or forsake her."

His prayers calmed her spirit. "Thank you."

"Now, what happened?"

"I just lost my job. I love my job. I've been here ten years." Her voice squeaked as she rambled.

"I don't know where you are, but do you want me to come and get you?"

"No, I'm outside Genesis Media Group—my *former* employer." She sobbed, then eventually composed herself. "But I can drive home."

"I know where that place is. Meet me in Forest Park in twenty minutes…"

Forest Park? Tally frowned. "Why? Forest Park is huge."

Minister Morgan chuckled. "I know. It's bigger than Central Park. How about in front of the Missouri History Museum—the entrance facing Lindell?"

"O-okay." She was not in the mood for crowds. Tally would rather hide and eat ice cream like the heartbroken do in the movies.

"You sure you can drive?"

"Yes." She had no choice. Plus, she needed to leave the parking lot before some of her former coworkers saw her and mocked her faith in God. She was always positive and encouraging, and Tally was sure some would get pleasure in her misery.

She drove away, not knowing what destiny lay before her. When she arrived at the history museum and parked, Tally called him as she walked to the entrance. When she looked up, Minister Morgan stood from the steps where he was sitting in a suit and tie. He held a bunch of balloons with happy faces and a cool snow cone.

Minister Morgan walked toward Tally, meeting her halfway. He hugged her without asking for permission. She didn't protest. It was comforting.

When she stepped out of his embrace, Tally eyed the dozen or so balloons. "Did you buy out the store?"

"I left them a few." He chuckled. "These are for us to give away."

"Huh?" She squinted. "Give away? And here I thought they were to cheer me up."

"They are. Since giving is more blessed than receiving, we can hand them out to the children."

His thoughtfulness was mind-boggling. This man was the perfect package for any woman in or outside the church. Tally smiled despite her circumstances. "Why are you still single?" she heard herself ask. "Sorry."

His eyes seemed to twinkle as he proceeded to hand out the balloons. "Well, I have to ask the right sister in the church, and she has to say yes. That's the short answer."

Tally didn't want to hear the long answer. She didn't know why she asked the question. A little girl approached, wanting a balloon. "Here you go, sweetie."

"Tell the lady thank you," the girl's mother prompted.

"Thank you."

That did make Tally feel good.

"So…" Minister Morgan came to her side with two balloons left, "when I first asked you out, you mentioned you weren't ready for a relationship. Were you delivered from a bad one?"

She shook her head and smiled as a little boy pointed to her balloon. Tally waited for him and his father to come closer. "Oh no. It was perfect until the Lord showed me it wasn't perfect to Him and deadly to my soul. The fear of hell caused me to surrender."

"You're brave to walk away from an unequally yoked relationship."

"God gave me a warning, so I had no choice if I didn't want to die in my sins."

Tally was relieved when Minister Morgan didn't continue the subject. Talking about Randall was just as sad as losing her job. It wasn't long before they were empty-handed and slurped on their snow cones.

"Ready to go inside?"

"Sure." While they strolled through the Seeking St. Louis exhibit, Tally was drawn to the galleries that traced the timeline of local disasters like the cholera outbreak, fires, and even the end of slavery. Surprisingly, it was fascinating.

They wandered from one exhibit to another as if Minister Morgan didn't have a job waiting for him to return, but encouraged Tally to speak whatever was on her mind. He was a good listener.

His facial expressions gave nothing away about what he was thinking. Once they reached the end of the Reflections gallery on sports, music, human rights and more, Minister Morgan asked, "Remember when I told you angels surrounded you during the shut-in prayer service?"

"Yes."

"You're on God's radar. I know you liked your job, but God has better opportunities. You'll have to trust His Will is perfect."

He took her hand and prayed. "Jesus, increase her faith in You." Then he looked at her. "Remember, whatever we think goes right or wrong in our lives, God isn't at fault. He removes things from our lives to give us better things."

Tally was quiet as she considered his words. "I guess."

"Now, how about a matinee—something funny?"

"You don't have to return to work?" Tally hoped not because she enjoyed his company.

"Nope. I took off." He smiled.

"I'd like that."

Chapter Nine

*I must work the works of him that sent me while it is day
the night comes when no man can work.* —John 9:4

Jude stayed close to Tally for the next few weeks but from
afar. He prayed with her and listened as she shared her
concerns about her financial security.

"It's been a game changer. I was able to watch my clients'
businesses grow. Some of those clients are members of our
church today because I witnessed Jesus' love for them, and two
surrendered to His salvation," she said.

The Lord revealed to him in a dream that Tally would face
an even bigger trial than losing her job, and prayer and fasting
would be essential for the upcoming spiritual battle.

Jude prayed even harder. He strolled into an office supply
store to drop off his laptop when he passed a familiar face, then
backtracked.

"Randall?" he asked the man who stood at the counter,
waiting to be serviced.

Turning around, the man frowned with a "Do I know you?"
expression.

"We've seen each other a few times. The barbershop and at
Christ For All Church. Jude Morgan, remember?"

"The minister," Randall mumbled, then nodded. "Right."

"I was hoping you would visit again, but I haven't seen
you." Jude was careful in his tone that it didn't sound accusatory
to put him on the defensive.

"Don't take this the wrong way, being a minister and all, but I'm not that into the church." He shrugged with no conviction. "Keeping it real."

"I see. Well, God calls everyone to the table to be fed." Jude paused. "Remember, even the Lord's invitations have an expiration date."

With his back to the counter, Randall leaned on his elbows as if he was making himself comfortable. He *hmphed.* "I'm not big on sitting for hours, reading my Bible, or giving up things that a mere man says are taboo. I don't want to live life in a straitjacket."

He has no idea how much freedom he has in Christ, Jude thought. "Don't miss out on living your best life because you're looking at a building instead of at God. Pastor Rodney's message is forty minutes—tops. The Bible is our spiritual food. God will hide His Word in your heart so you won't want to sin against Him, and despite the devil's propaganda campaign, living for Christ gives us liberty. I've been walking for Jesus for years, and I don't feel deprived. Your sister and brother-in-law enjoy the benefits of Christ."

Irritation seemed to build in Randall. Jude had to tread lightly, but sometimes a person didn't get second and third chances, so he had to work when presented with the opportunity.

"If I think I need more of Jesus, I'll come back to visit, and I'll look for you, Minister," Randall said with finality in his voice and walked away.

"Please call me Jude." He took the hint. "Don't let it be said too late." He was certain Omega had planted the seed in her brother's heart. Randall refused to let Jude water it.

Pray for him! God thundered.

Jude turned around, and Randall was gone as if he was never there. Jude stepped outside.

No one was in the parking lot.

Coming back inside, Randall had vanished. Where did the man go?

Satan, you are a liar. In the name of Jesus, I am pulling down the stronghold you have on Randall Addams' life.

Jude checked-in his computer for service, then walked out of the store, annoyed, until Tally's ringtone made him smile.

Randall reviewed the posters he'd had the office supply store create for his IT company's free after-school computer classes. He partnered with two fraternity brothers who also owned and operated Black businesses. Together, they donated sixty laptops for school-age children.

The event was Tally's brainchild three years earlier as a way for his company, Tech Problems Solved, to help Black businesses get more public exposure.

"Plus, charity contributions are tax write-offs," she had told him. Tally had added free five extra commercials to his advertising campaign for the event as a first-time customer.

Tally had been good for him. Everything about her. Randall had thought he had been good to her and for her too. She was incredibly smart and engaging. Tally asked for so little in their relationship, which made him want to give her the world. So many good memories swirled in his head as he turned his chair to stare out the office window behind him. Randall wanted private space to savor the good times whenever he thought about her. Tally had touched every part of his life.

"I miss you, baby." He wished his whispers would reach her ears.

Randall hadn't seen any warning signs that would lead her to abruptly want out of their relationship as if what they shared hadn't mattered. For what? God?

It didn't make sense. Randall frowned and rubbed his freshly shaven jaw, which Tally liked to caress. The crater she had created in his heart when she left remained unsealed, even after more than a year. Although he missed Tally more than anything and she had him wrapped around her slender finger, Randall was his own man. His sisters, Omega and Delta, called him stubborn to a fault.

Church wasn't his thing.

Not even to make her happy.

He tried to recover from his gloom by going out on a few dates. Brittani was first, then there was Ciara. Felicia had been the longest fling at a month.

Felicia had been woman enough to tell him to come back whenever he was over Tally since her name had come up too many times in their conversation.

"We can pick up where we left off—if I'm still interested and available." She hadn't blinked saying it.

To date, he hadn't called her back. And wouldn't.

Clearing his throat, Randall turned back to his computer. He had a business to run, profits to make, and staff to pay. His workplace philosophy was to keep livelihood separate from lifestyle challenges.

His heart defied him. Thoughts of Tally lingered. Her free consultation for his business success still worked. Randall had refused to accept her explanation for the breakup. Whenever they disagreed on anything, they would talk it out.

They couldn't be more compatible. They loved to dance, support charities, watch movies, travel…the list was endless. His sisters envied what he and Tally had. "Now, who has the last laugh?" he said about his younger sister getting married first.

Tally stopped taking his calls months after they—she—ended their relationship.

That hurt.

No, it angered him. He took the hint.

With the upcoming company event, Randall had a reason to call Tally at work. "This will be a business call, Miss Gilbert."

As he was about to look up the main number for Genesis Media Group, his HR head, Madison Hill, knocked on his door.

"Randall, got a minute?" She didn't look happy, which meant he wouldn't be happy either.

"Sure." He pointed to a chair in front of his desk.

She closed the door and flopped in the seat, clutching papers. "I have a garnishment letter to withhold earnings on Welton Tipton."

Randall huffed and rubbed his forehead. He paid his fifty-three employees above-average wages to retain them so that they could live comfortably. Welton was one of his top software designers and troubleshooters.

"Reason?" He tapped his finger on his desk. He didn't have time for a money management lecture.

"He defaulted on a personal loan—a big amount." Sadness filled her eyes. "I guess you never know what a person is going through behind closed doors. I thought he was stingy because he never chipped in for get-well cards, raffles, or anything. My pastor told us to pray for others." She *tsk*ed.

Welton needs more than prayer, but he kept those thoughts to himself. "Okay. Thanks, Maddy, for letting me know."

He was quiet after she left. Randall started his IT firm for financial freedom to pay himself and others their worth. He knew all of his employees and some of their spouses. That's where it ended. He didn't know their children's names, ages, et cetera.

Madison had all that in her files. He required her to alert him concerning personnel issues where finances or destructive behaviors could negatively affect the company's image.

Money problems bothered Randall. Desperate people could kill or steal for it.

Regrouping, Randall cleared his head and reached for his desk phone. He typed KMJT radio into the search engine and called the number.

"Good morning. Genesis Media Group," the unfamiliar woman answered.

"Tally Gilbert, please." His heart pounded, preparing to be wowed by her sultry voice.

"I'm sorry. She's no longer employed here. Can I connect you to the sales director for assistance?"

The phone almost slipped out of his hand. What? Randall held his breath, then exhaled. He shook his head to make sure he'd heard right. "*Ahhh*, how long has she been gone?"

"Sorry, sir. I'm not sure. I'll connect you to the sales department."

Randall disconnected the call. He didn't need to buy ad space. That was just a rouse, but he would have. When had Tally left, and why? She loved that job. What had happened? Who knew? If they were still together, she would have discussed her decision with him. That's what they did. They were each other's confidant.

He called his sister.

"Hey, big brother," Omega answered cheerfully while talking to someone in the background. "Okay, Reba. We'll talk later. Thanks for sharing that testimony with me. God is awesome."

He was too discombobulated for pleasantries. "Did you know Tally no longer works for the radio station?"

"Yeah. She told Mitchell and me a few weeks ago."

"What? Weeks ago?" Randall tried to tame his roar. "Why didn't anyone tell me?"

"Why should we? You two aren't dating anymore, so calm down, Big Bad Wolf."

"Because I still care about her." He stated the obvious. "Does she need any money? Does she have another job?" he rambled off the questions as they came to him.

"Bro, as far as I know, she hasn't landed anything else yet. The company cut staff. She made a lot of money and was the first to go."

Randall internally went on the defensive. Tally Gilbert was top in sales for years. They let the cream of the crop go.

You let her go, a whisper stopped him.

No, she left on her own, Randall argued.

"Of course, she was down, but we're praying she'll bounce back soon."

Fuming inside, Randall gritted his teeth in frustration. "That's not good enough. You know I have little patience for waiting."

Omega grunted. "The whole world knows."

"I have to help her. I'll give her something until she finds something."

"Bro, she won't take it. Mitchell and I tried to give her a love offering, and if Mother Kincaid from our church wasn't talking with her, Tally would have turned it down. God has a blessing for her better than the blessing she had. Think about that."

Randall cleared his throat. "Is there supposed to be a message for me in between the lines?"

"I'll let you simmer on that. I've got to go, bro. Tally will be fine. God has her back."

"And so do I." He ended the call first.

The question was how he would give her money without her knowing it was from him.

What else had changed that no one had told him about? Randall left work early.

Destination: Tally's house.

Game plan?

No idea.

Chapter Ten

Peace I leave with you, my peace I give unto you: not as the world
giveth, give I unto you. Let not your heart be troubled,
neither let it be afraid. —John 14:27

Tally was accustomed to giving to charity, not *being* the
charity. First, Omega and Mitchell had forced her to take a
hundred dollars when she confided to them that Genesis Media
had let her go. Her eyes had misted, but at least she didn't cry as
reality started to sink in.

Mother Kincaid decided she wanted in on the blessing, so
she had those on the morning prayer line bless Tally if they
could afford to give.

The church mother had endeared herself as a grandmother
figure to Tally and Porsha who were deprived of as small girls.
Mother Kincaid had even set up a CashApp account and
collected three hundred dollars. Tally's heart warmed at people's
generosity.

Minister Morgan blessed her in invaluable ways, too,
praying for her faith not to fail. He encouraged her to believe
God's plan for her. He was a spiritual drill sergeant, but she
needed his encouragement.

His texts throughout the day with Scriptures and occasional
flowers had wormed his way into a special place in her heart. He
wasn't a bad catch if she was mentally and emotionally free.

She praised Jesus for her brothers and sisters in Christ for
their support. Jude had even been speaking with the HR

department at Boeing. Although the aerospace company offered competitive salaries, Tally wasn't sure she was a good fit.

One evening, Tally returned home after visiting Sinclaire to see an envelope slipped under her door. A wad of hundred-dollar bills was stuffed inside. No name, but Tally knew the sender.

Randall.

A hint of his cologne was unmistakable. Her heart throbbed for his affection—the hugs alone would make everything alright in her world. His kisses were not only deadly but sinful because they led to the bedroom. Immediately, she shut down those images with the Scripture from 2 Corinthians 10:5: *Casting down imaginations and every high thing that exalts itself against the knowledge of God, bringing every thought into captivity to the obedience of Christ.*

She closed her eyes and held the envelope next to her chest. "Lord, please save Randall, not just because I love him, but for himself." A tear fell.

I will draw him, God whispered.

When? It had already been over a year. She sighed.

I never break my promises.

Then she recalled Minister Morgan's prayer for her to increase her faith.

Tally tried not to worry. Mother Kincaid would take her to task for it. The church mother had begun an active prayer request during the morning prayer chain as she listened to their specific requests on her behalf.

"Lord, give her the position You want her to have. Bless her in every way. Supply her needs like you feed the sparrows in the air," one prayer member prayed.

"Father God, speak her job into existence. Only You have that power for Your Word not to return to You without accomplishing what You set it out to do," Mother Kincaid had added.

"Don't give up, Sister Gilbert," said Lisa, a newcomer to the prayer line.

"Don't worry, prayer warriors. When we pray, we believe God. Remember, our faith affects miracles and healings," Mother Kincaid said at the end of the hour and cited passages in the New Testament that said as much. "Lord, don't let faith hinder Your work in me." Throughout the day she memorized and quoted Matthew 13:58 and Mark 6:5.

―――――― ∽ ――――――

Friday morning, Sinclaire dropped Carlton off at school. She was sad to learn Tally lost her job, yet she never stopped sending Carlton home after church with Sunday dinner for the family.

That was kindness Sinclaire never knew. She had also seen a change in Carlton. After four days into the school year, he didn't want to go, which surprised her. Her son was a straight-A student. When he came home, he ran to his room to pray, sometimes for almost an hour.

Something was up.

Sinclaire walked into his bedroom with the intent to stop him, but she couldn't proceed. It was as if the power of God filled the room and had consumed her son on a mountaintop.

Hearing her son pray in a heavenly language made her curious. It wasn't drugs, voodoo, or gibberish. She felt a spiritual presence that didn't make her afraid. Just curious.

This morning, she sensed a calmness about him while she suffered another terrible night. The dreams of her son disappearing from school continued to nag at her, but she was clueless about what it meant and what she was supposed to do about it.

Sinclaire followed her daily routine and drove Carlton to school. Parked at the entrance, she squinted, then blinked to focus. What looked like a funnel cloud was headed toward the school. It was massive, and Sinclaire was too struck with fear to move or scream.

As powerful as it was, it didn't destroy anything in its path surprisingly, then it seemed to swirl around her son.

Did this have anything to do with her dreams or his prayers? Was her son about to disappear? Released from whatever held her back, Sinclaire hurried out of her car, leaving the small ones strapped in the backseat. "Carlton," she called.

He looked over his shoulder and waved. "It's okay, Mom. They're here to protect me."

They? Who are they? And from what?

Her question was answered when what had appeared as a cloud separated to resemble soldiers.

Carlton turned back around and continued walking inside. Sinclaire didn't know what to make of it as she stared. She got back into her car and called Tally. She answered right away. "Can you meet me at my house?"

"Sure. Are you okay? Are the children?"

"Just come, please." Sinclaire disconnected and noticed her hands were shaking. She glanced in the backseat. Both of her children were awake, alert, and watching her.

Sinclaire returned to her apartment and paced the floor while waiting. Sissy played with her baby brother until the doorbell rang.

When she opened the door, Sinclaire collapsed in Tally's arms. She sobbed, afraid of what she saw.

"Hey. What's going on? You sounded upset over the phone. Are the children okay?" Tally scanned the room, then hugged the children.

"I hope so." Sinclaire led Tally into the kitchen and sat at the counter for privacy but where she could keep an eye on TJ and Sissy.

Sinclaire spoke softly. "I was so scared. I don't know if this is connected or not, but I've been having these bad dreams about Carlton, and Carlton has been coming home praying. This morning, when I dropped him off at school, I thought a funnel cloud was racing toward the building. It was ferocious, but everything around it was calm and untouched..."

She sniffed as she relived the scene. Her voice cracked. "Is my son going to die in a funnel cloud? Is that why he's disappearing from his classroom in my dreams?"

Tally reached for Sinclaire's hands, bowed her head, and began to pray. "Jesus, please calm this mother's troubled spirit. You saved Carlton for Your purpose. In Jesus' name. Amen." Looking up, she met Sinclaire's eyes. "I'm not a Bible scholar, but I think your son is in good hands. From the instances I've read in the Bible, it's a good sign. Jesus is coming back in a cloud to redeem his people. That's when Carlton and the other saints will disappear in the air."

"I don't want my baby to go to heaven without me."

"Then, it's between you and the Lord. You have to repent and be baptized for the remission of your sins. Whatever Carlton has been going through at school, he has taken it to God in prayer. God is responding. It's going to be okay."

How could this woman be so calm? Sinclaire was traumatized. Her hands shook as she wiped her face. She inhaled and exhaled.

Sinclaire collapsed on a nearby stool and attempted to compose herself as her other children watched. "Okay, okay. First, let me comprehend that you are saying that Carlton is okay."

"He is better than okay, sis. Trust God." Tally smiled and patted her hand. it was comforting.

"I guess you're right about a lot of things, Tally. I hate to be wrong, but I am. I need rest at night and don't want to keep worrying about my finances and children."

"I'm glad."

"Whew! I feel so defeated. Since I don't have any projects today, I should continue job hunting. I guess you, too, huh?" Tally was more unemployed than Sinclaire. At least she had projects, just not enough of them coming in right now.

"God is supplying my needs, despite the rejection or no responses from the places where I applied. God is moving pieces for me. And He will do the same for you if you go to Jesus. All He wants is your attention, and He can take it from there."

Sinclaire peeped into the living room to check on Sissy and TJ. "You make it sound so simple."

"Salvation is. It's life that's complicated. Come on. Let's take the children to the park. We both can use some fresh air."

"Okay." Sinclaire wasn't a trusting person. She had been burned when she let her guard down, but Tally had proven to be a friend to her family. Could Sinclaire trust God with her son?

As Sinclaire packed a bag, Carlton's school sent a mass text, notifying the parents that two students in his second grade had brought weapons to class.

"No," she screamed.

Tally and the children raced to the kitchen. "What's wrong?"

"Children brought weapons to Carlton's school." She continued reading the text. "The authorities were notified, and the students involved were removed from the property. All the children are okay." Sinclaire exhaled. Tears streamed down her face. "They're safe. I'm sorry for doubting the Lord. I need to feel Jesus' protection!"

Tally began to praise God, and soon Sissy and the toddler mimicked her. Sinclaire wasn't expecting to hear God speak in a language she couldn't understand, but she felt the intensity of its power.

"Ask, and you shall receive." Tally clapped as she smiled through happy tears. "All you need is the baptism in Jesus' name, and you're set for eternal life."

Whatever power and peace she experienced just now, Sinclaire didn't want to let it go. "Do I have to wait until Sunday to get baptized?"

"Nope. Minister Morgan said our ministers will open the doors for anyone any time who wants to repent and be baptized in Jesus' name."

Once Sinclaire composed herself, she faced Tally. "Make the call. First, I want to get my son from school."

———————— ⌒ ————————

Carlton would be ecstatic.

When she picked him up from school, she hugged him like he was a toddler again. "Thank God you're alright." She squeezed him again.

"Mom, I can't breathe." He wiggled out of her embrace.

"Sorry. Were you scared?" Sinclaire asked, patting his face. He looked so brave.

"No. Those boys were bad, and they made other people bad and mean to me. I asked God to help me. Jesus sent angels, and the other kids saw them too. It was cool." Carlton grinned, looking so much like his deadbeat father. That was another situation she was in the process of correcting.

One tear fell, then another down Sinclaire's cheek. "Come on. We're on our way to church."

"You?" His eyes bucked, and he stepped back.

"Yes. Today I'm going to get my sins washed away. Miss Gilbert stopped by to visit. I repented, and I heard the Lord speaking through me in a language I don't think is spoken on this earth. Miss Gilbert said the Lord had filled me with His Holy Spirit. I'm on my way to the church to get baptized. I thought you might want to be there."

"Thank You, Jesus!" He jumped in place while pumping his fist in the air, then raced to the car. "Come on, Mom. Let's go."

Sinclaire had never been this eager to get to church. The pastor, Tally, and two other men—one who looked familiar—stood outside the church door waiting for her.

Tally and one man walked to Sinclaire's car and helped get the children.

"Sinclaire, you remember Minister Morgan," Tally said as she lifted Sissy from the back seat.

Tilting her head, Sinclaire studied him. "Oh, yes. Carlton can't stop talking about you. Thank you."

"It's an honor to have him at our church. Thank you for letting him come. Now, it's time to finish your salvation journey," Minister Morgan said with the kindest eyes.

Sinclaire trailed them inside the church and followed Tally down a hall to a changing room. Two other women had come at this short notice. They had interrupted their day to be there for her. Sinclaire was overcome with emotions as she fought back the tears. *I matter.*

She faced Tally. "Thank you for everything—from being a friend to being here and like a sister to me."

Tally hugged her. "We are sister-friends. Now, we're about to become sisters in Christ. And imagine *if* I were working, I'd have missed your rebirth."

"Tally called us. We weren't going to miss your day of salvation. Remember me? We met at community day. I'm Mother Kincaid." She hugged Sinclaire, then started singing, "Take Me to the Water" until Sinclaire finished changing her clothes. She donned a white T-shirt, gown, socks, and a swim cap.

People had caused the church hurt to drive Sinclaire away, but God placed people in her life who didn't know her but were demonstrating church love.

"I'm ready!" Sinclaire grinned and lifted her arms in the air. When she entered the pool, Minister Morgan stretched out his hand. She looked back at Tally who nodded.

With Minister Morgan guiding her, she stepped down into the water. From the other side of the pool's transparent glass wall, Carlton held his baby brother while Sissy stood next to two older women.

"Have you repented of your sins?" the minister asked.

"Yes."

He lifted his hand. "My dear sister, upon the confession of your faith and the confidence you have in the blessed Word of God, concerning His death, burial, and Grand Resurrection, I now indeed baptize you in the name of our Lord Jesus Christ for the remission of your sins. No other name in heaven or on earth is as great as the name of Jesus given for our salvation."

Minister Morgan's grip on the neck of her clothing was firm as he submerged her. Sinclaire came out fighting with the water. It was as if a supernatural power was unleashed. The minister made a great effort to hold her steady as she stepped out of the pool rejoicing.

The moment was surreal. Sinclaire couldn't describe her emotions after baptism. Such a simple yet forceful thing. She felt different.

Sinclaire's eyes were opened to her spiritual being. God had become more than her Creator who she thought was unreachable. Jesus was real. She had the evidence to prove it when she heard Him speaking through her, then saw the funnel cloud that protected her son. After today, nobody could convince her otherwise.

She laughed at herself. Why did she make so much fuss about not stepping foot into the church? Jesus was who she needed all along, not a man.

Once she had changed back into her clothes and walked into the sanctuary where a dozen people waited for her, Sinclaire received a hearty applause as if she were a celebrity. The pastor praised the Lord. "A soul has been removed from Satan's hit list. Hallelujah," he shouted at the top of his lungs.

The small gathering danced and praised God as Sinclaire listened to the Lord fill her mouth with a heavenly language.

Tears streamed down her cheeks as she worshipped the Lord with her dance. Sissy and Carlton danced with her. When she was back in control, Sinclaire grinned and shook her head. "Why did I take so long to come to Jesus?"

"God's timing is perfect. Some folks come with His whisper. Others come kicking and screaming," Pastor Rodney said.

Sinclaire raised her hand sheepishly. "That was me."

"Doesn't matter. The first shall be last, and the last first. Here's a new Bible for you to feast on your Scriptures," Minister Morgan said, gently presenting it to Sinclaire as if it were a newborn baby. "Hold on to the Word of God for dear life. It's precious."

"I will." Sinclaire nodded, hugging the Bible to her chest.

"Does this mean Miss Gilbert won't pick me up for church anymore?" Carlton asked. His blank expression didn't tell Sinclaire whether he was happy or disappointed.

"We will come as a family, son, and we can see Minister Morgan and Miss Gilbert at church. Is that okay?" She watched her son's expression. His eyes lit as he grinned.

Tally draped her arm around Sinclaire's shoulders and squeezed. "I'm going to miss picking Carlton up, but I'd rather see all of you here at church."

"Amen," Mother Kincaid chimed in.

Minister Morgan chuckled. "You two could pass as sisters."

Sinclaire faced Tally. "We are sisters for real now."

"Yep, in Christ." Tally stepped back so Sinclaire could receive hugs and personal congratulations from everyone there.

That night at home, Sinclaire didn't want to go to bed. The nightmares that taunted her had nothing to do with it. If the Bible was spiritual food, she couldn't get enough of it as she read the Word for the first time in a long while.

In her prayers, she thanked God for His patience while she got her act together. "Lord, I'm going to trust You for the right job to take care of my family, in Jesus' name. Amen."

Saturday morning, Sinclaire took the children to Marshalls department store to get a few things. While she scrutinized children's clothing in the clearance section, her son inched away, closer to a stranger.

"Don't do it," she overheard Carlton tell a man who looked like he could crush her son with his fist. He was huge in size.

The man frowned at her son. "You don't know what you're talking about."

Me neither, Sinclaire thought as she was about to get Carlton. In a blink of an eye, the customer snatched a stack of shoe boxes and hurried out of the store without paying for them.

"Carlton, what's going on?" Sinclaire was bewildered at what just happened.

"Mom, I told him not to steal, but he did anyway." Her son was so upset that he was on the verge of tears.

The employees scrambled into action, calling the police while customers who had witnessed the heist, stared in disbelief.

"Hallelujah!" escaped from Sinclaire's lips at the realization the man could have had a gun or injured Carlton. Yes, she served a God who protects.

No longer interested in shopping, Sinclaire gathered her family and left. That was enough excitement for one day.

Later that night, Sinclaire was in good spirits as she got the children's clothes ready for church the next day, then a news report caught her attention.

"A police crash in North County leaves two suspects dead and two in critical condition," anchor Lee Newman said, "Police say they were pursuing a vehicle wanted in a carjacking when that car slammed into another car, killing the driver. Authorities later learned that the other car was fleeing the scene of a robbery at Marshalls department store."

Sinclaire's heart pounded. It was the same man her son had told not to steal. Now, that man was either dead or in critical condition.

Pray for sinners, God whispered.

"Lord, let him repent and not die in his sins." She said a brief prayer but wondered if he was worthy after the bad stuff he'd done.

I died for all sinners such as you, God said.

Sinclaire thought about her lifestyle outside of Christ's will, which yielded three children. No, she couldn't judge anybody. She got back on her knees and prayed for the survivors because their souls depended on it.

Chapter Eleven

...but this one thing I do, forgetting those things which are behind, and reaching forth unto those things which are before. I press toward the mark for the prize of the high calling of God in Christ Jesus.
—Philippians 3:13–14

On Sunday morning, Tally was speechless after Sinclaire shared what happened yesterday while she and the children were at the store.

Mother Kincaid *tsk*ed. "The Bible says in Joel two and twenty that '*God will pour out His spirit upon all flesh, and your sons and your daughters shall prophesy, your old men shall dream dreams, your young men shall see visions.*'"

The woman squinted at Carlton as if she knew something Sinclaire didn't. "Sounds like your young man was operating in the Holy Ghost with a revelation from God. Whatever you do, don't hinder his spiritual growth." Mother Kincaid hugged Carlton. "It means something to walk with Jesus, especially at an early age. It keeps us out of trouble later in life. And when trouble does come, we're protected. Even while those young men were in their sins, Christ died for the ungodly."

Sinclaire nodded. "God told me to pray for them, even though they were the ones who were in the wrong. I did but didn't understand."

"The wisest person on earth can't understand God's doing. When Cain murdered his brother, the Lord protected him with a mark to keep others from hurting Cain."

"Go figure." Tally shrugged. "My thoughts definitely aren't God's, for sure."

"Wow." Sinclaire shook her head. "Doesn't make sense to me either."

"One day." Mother Kincaid smiled, then they entered the sanctuary together. "We'll see about getting some young ministers to help mentor Brother Carlton."

"Minister Morgan can. He likes me." Carlton beamed.

Tally patted the boy's shoulder. "True. We all love you, and as you can see, Sinclaire, folks are loving on you and your children." Her heart swelled with happiness. Her circle of new converts was growing. One person remained missing.

When she first came to Christ For All Church, it was Omega, Mitchell, her, April and Caylee. Then Mitchell's parents surrendered, and they filled up a row. Tally's sister and parents repented and were baptized, Now, she would make room for Sinclaire and her family.

The worship was high in the spirit, and Sinclaire joined in as if she had been a member all along. When Pastor Rodney stood at the podium on the pulpit, he recognized visitors and new converts. Sinclaire and a few others stood to a roar of applause.

"Amen." Pastor Rodney clapped along with the congregation. "My message today is the entire Bible." He lifted his. "This is the living, breathing Word of God. It's powerful to raise the dead, heal the sick, rebuke demons that cause them to tremble, forgive sins and speak His will into existence." He paused. "Remember, only God can speak His Word, and it happens. We can't create a world or give someone life. Through prophecy, God uses us to speak." He cited numerous Scriptures, which Tally jotted down: James 2:19, Romans 4:17–19, and Matthew 10:8.

After three baptisms and the benediction, Minister Morgan approached Tally and her family from the other side of the sanctuary from where he sat in the front.

He greeted everyone with a hearty "Praise the Lord."

"Where is Sister Sinclaire and Brother Carlton?" He squinted, scanning the sanctuary.

"She left right after the benediction. TJ was fussy," Tally explained. This man was not only handsome, kind, and thoughtful, now she had another adjective to describe his character—genuinely concerned about the new saints. Tally would relay that message to Sinclaire so she would know that people did care about her, not her past.

"Minister Morgan, you're welcome to come to our home for dinner, say around three," Cynthia, Tally's mother, said. She had been a fan of his since he nurtured Tally emotionally and spiritually after her layoff.

"I accept." Minister Morgan's eyes brightened as if he was given a popsicle. He waited while her mother scribbled her address on the back of a bulletin, then handed it to him.

"See you then. Thank you, Mother Gilbert."

"My pleasure." Her mother's eyes sparkled with mischief as a potential matchmaker.

So that's why her parents were hanging around in the sanctuary. Usually, they were the first to leave.

When Minister Morgan was out of ear range, Porsha didn't hold back her giggles.

Tally elbowed her. "Not funny. I was ambushed."

"I thought you two were becoming close." Her mother's innocent look didn't work on Tally.

"Yes, in the close friend/prayer partner category. Mom, I can't believe I was set up. Dad, you let your wife invite another man into your home?" Tally lifted a brow at the woman with whom she shared her height and resemblance.

Her family had hinted more than once that it was time for Tally to date some of the eligible bachelors in the church. They hand-picked their first candidate.

He grinned. "Minister Morgan definitely isn't coming to see my wife. He's sweet on you." Her father winked and hugged her. "I know Randall was your first love, but he's not here."

She reminded herself that more often than she wanted to admit, but coming from her parents made it sound hopeless. But they were wrong about Randall being her first love. He was her only love.

Now God reminded her every morning that He is love.

"Porsha, were you in on this?" Tally feigned hurt and betrayal.

"I…I knew they were scheming—more Mama. I didn't know she had come up with a plan."

Tally rolled her eyes. She couldn't protest too hard. Minister Morgan was a well-mannered and good-looking man, but she was more attracted to the spiritual part of him.

Mitchell and Omega had been prayer partners until something changed between them and the pair became a couple. Tally saw more developing between them from the beginning while they were clueless. Did her family see something with Minister Morgan that Tally didn't?

She needed a job, not romance.

The sisters separated and would meet at their parents' home. Once there, Porsha wanted to keep the romantic conversation going while they were in the kitchen helping to prepare for their guest.

Tally shut down that conversation and cleared her throat. "After this morning's message, I'm believing God to speak His will in my life about a j-o-b."

"With your résumé, you won't have a problem," her father assured her from his perch on the stool, watching the ladies buzz around the kitchen.

"Thanks, Dad. I just signed up with several recruiters. One of them said I won't be on the market long."

"Sounds like that could pertain to your love life too. Minister Morgan is a nice young man." Her mother smiled.

Tally groaned and wanted to pull out the curls in her hair in frustration. "You do remember I ended the love life I had when I surrendered to Christ?"

"How could any of us forget?" Her father chuckled. "That was a shocker. But I hope you're not holding out for Randall. I like him and how he treated you, but if he isn't going to get on board with his salvation, I don't want you to pass up good men—one in particular."

He kissed her cheek, then headed toward the family room to relax since he wasn't helping anyway.

Tally trailed him, claiming a spot on the sofa and tucking her legs under her skirt. "Daddy, if Randall surrendered today and asked me to marry him tomorrow, I would. But I know my ex. Randall is his own man, and not one to follow the leader. I believe God will bless me with a husband according to what I need and want." She paused. "A part of me is holding out—"

"I knew it!" Cynthia said.

"I said a part of me. I love Randall, Mom. The Bible says there is a season for everything. I'm just waiting for my season of loving Randall to end. Please respect my process."

Porsha nodded. "That was deep, sis. I'm glad you know someone is out there, and he could be walking in the door soon."

"Just don't shut Minister Morgan down," her father said. "He respects you, and I like that."

Then why did two other women he dated jump ship and marry someone else? Tally wondered but didn't repeat her private conversation with Mother Kincaid.

He has a purpose in your life, God whispered.

———————— ∞ ————————

Jude arrived at the Gilbert family home five minutes earlier than expected. His mother had trained him on the proper protocol when visiting a woman friend and her family. Flowers. Smile. Fresh breath.

Brother and Sister Gilbert treated him like their favorite son—considering they didn't have one—when they welcomed him at the door.

Porsha's smile was more engaging than Tally's, which was cordial. How these sisters were single before they came to Christ For All Church and even now was unbelievable.

Thick lashes drew Jude's attention to Tally's hazel eyes. Her best asset was a toss-up—her eyes or that smile, which she rarely gave him, but Jude had glimpsed it on the woman she favored—her mother.

Porsha was almost a replica of Tally with her pretty eyes, but her smile lacked dimples, and her hair was shoulder-length.

At the dinner table, Brother Gilbert asked him to bless their food, then the questions swirled as serving dishes passed hands.

"Minister Morgan," Tally's father addressed him despite his insistence they call him Jude, "tell me about your family."

Tally used his title, too, and never crossed it. Jude appreciated her respect. Some women, including decoys in the church, wanted to tempt him to fall into sin. "I have a younger brother who is also unmarried. My parents have been married for thirty-nine years. I'm thirty-seven, and we all have a solid, loving relationship."

Jude was accustomed to being in the hot seat when mothers tried to match him with their daughters, nieces, or neighbors, but this time, Jude wanted to impress Tally more than her family.

"My daughter said you worked at Boeing. What do you do there?" Sister Gilbert asked.

Glad that Tally had passed on that tidbit, he was encouraged that she had been talking about him. "I've been there for ten years. I'm a software engineer," Jude divulged and waited for the next set of questions that involved his personal life. He counted down three…two…

"You mentioned one time you've been at Christ For All Church for five years," Porsha said instead of her mother. "Unless you're divorced, how come you haven't married?"

"God hasn't revealed my other heartbeat. Working in the ministry for the Lord requires sacrifices and a partner willing to work on the spiritual battlefield. That woman has to be called to do that."

Tally's mother cleared her throat. "You know God has given my Tally special gifts to win souls for Jesus."

Nodding with a snicker, Jude glanced at Tally with admiration. "I'm aware."

Jude guessed he passed inspection because Brother Gilbert talked sports until the plates were cleared.

Sister Gilbert's mac and cheese won him over at the dinner, along with her meatloaf, string beans, and hot rolls. "Everything was delicious," he said, patting his stomach when he finished and wiping his mouth.

Tally and Porsha left the table to bring dessert from the kitchen—apple pie. Two hours later, Jude left with a covered plate—Sister Gilbert insisted, not taking no for an answer—and a hearty handshake from Brother Gilbert.

The sisters smiled and gave him the standard, "Praise the Lord." That was it.

In his car, Jude did a quick assessment. The Gilbert parents liked him, and so did Tally. But the dinner didn't help advance their friendship to another level. He had thought that was possible when she was laid off, and they talked more. Tally wasn't crossing the line, leaving him at a stalemate, back at the starting point. What did he have to do to win her over?

A few weeks later, while Jude was troubleshooting a program, he mumbled to himself out of nowhere when he thought about Tally. "God, can You clarify my purpose in her life?"

The Lord didn't answer, but Jude smiled when his phone rang. The image of their selfie flashed on his screen. "Hello."

"God did it, Minister Morgan!" She sniffed.

He smiled and waited to hear more.

"I can't believe it. I got a job offer paying me at least forty thousand dollars more than what I earned at Genesis Media."

"What?" That's an incredible raise. "Praise Jesus." Jude rejoiced with her over the phone. God had given her exceedingly more than she had prayed for or could think she was worth. "Let's celebrate."

"Exactly."

"When do you start?" Her excitement was contagious.

"I leave in three weeks."

"Leave? Where are you going?" Jude pressed pause on the celebration.

"Oh," she said, giggling. "I forgot to mention the position is in New York."

"New York," he repeated, lost for words. Yes, Jude had been praying alongside Tally for her blessing. He just assumed it would be in the Gateway City.

Tally became chatty. "I know, right? After telling my family, you were my second call. Now, I've got to call Mother Kincaid. She's been praying for me too…."

The excitement she pumped into him had imploded when Tally ended the call. Was there a change of plans, and Jude didn't get an update from the Lord? Now what?

Chapter Twelve

*The Lord will rescue me from every evil attack and will bring me
safely to his heavenly kingdom...* —2 Timothy 4:18

R andall strolled out of the grocery store close to his office
while talking with Logan on the phone. A ruckus across the
busy street snagged his attention.

"Hey, man. There are some fools out here arguing. Let me
go check it out before somebody gets hurt. See you tomorrow."

They had made plans to meet downtown after work for
happy hour.

"Make sure you're not that Good Samaritan who gets hurt,
bro," Logan said, then added, "Be safe."

"Will do." Randall threw his purchases in his car, then
hurried across the street to break them up. Bystanders filming the
worse of people rather than intervening or calling the police
irked him. A big guy overpowered a man with an onslaught of
punches, not giving the victim a chance to defend himself.

The man wouldn't survive more impacts. Randall shoved his
way through the crowd. "Excuse me. Excuse me."

No!

Randall froze in his steps. He tried to move but couldn't go
forward. Something restrained him, but no one held him.

You are outnumbered, God's voice thundered.

Where? Randall smirked. There were two men.

God opened his eyes to see three men sitting in a car at the
corner. Guns were pointed their way.

More was at stake than saving the underdog. Innocent bystanders could get hurt or killed. *Right.* He could probably rescue the man, but what about the onlookers?

Whipping out his phone, he dialed 9-1-1 and gave the location. If he couldn't help the victim, he refused to stand around and witness the slaughter.

Plus, he needed to keep an eye trained on the men in the car.

Within minutes, sirens blared in the background. The crowd scattered—even the bully ran in the opposite direction to get away. Randall stayed in the distance. He couldn't leave until he knew the man was alive and would be okay.

Later that night, Randall wondered about the man who lay bleeding on a lot. Although not a fan of crime recap, he turned on the ten o'clock news to learn what happened to the assault victim. Not surprisingly, but hoping for a better outcome, he learned the man had died of his injuries.

That hurt.

"Alive one minute and dead the next." He exhaled, clicked off the flat screen, and walked into the kitchen. Too early for bed and too late to snack.

The news had shaken him up and had his stomach twisted. He called Logan. His friend answered on the first ring. "Hey, remember that fight or beatdown I told you about earlier?"

"Yeah?"

"Dude died." Randall didn't know why he was so affected by a stranger's death, but he was. Maybe because he thought back to when his sister was in the crossfire of a shooting. Mitchell had protected Omega, but what if he hadn't? The Addams family would have been one person absent in a family photo. Tonight, it was somebody else who was mourning.

"I'm glad you're okay. Sometimes you have to stay out of foolery." Logan *tsk*ed. "Man, but I'm sorry to hear that."

"Yeah."

"Switching to better news—the game—another friend is joining us."

Randall was too mentally distracted to engage, so he listened. He wished he had intervened. Would God have shielded him the way Omega had said angels protected her?

He grunted. Randall still found that hard to believe. One thing he would never admit to Logan or anyone else was the voice he heard forbidding him from getting involved.

Randall wasn't expecting this news. It took a moment to digest. The bad news wasn't welcome. His morning was off to a good start. New clients had signed contracts with Tech Problems Solved, and Randall had a great weekend with his family. Omega and Mitchell had invited all of them over to their new home.

"You still there?" Logan asked over the phone.

"Yeah, man. I can't believe Brian is gone. He was at my sister's wedding, and I ran into him the day we were going to the game." He shivered at the thought of death snatching a life. "I mean, who has a heart attack at forty-two?"

Randall's friend Brian had. Life was short and unfair at times.

Although the two stayed in contact a couple of times a year, Randall considered Brian a big brother since he was three years older than him. They both pledged to Kappa Alpha Psi Fraternity, Incorporated. Randall's brotherhood was a sore spot with his father who pledged Omega Psi Phi. Randall had planned to follow in his father's footsteps, then changed his mind and refused to back down. He never regretted his decision.

Rubbing his head, Randall thought about regrets. His heart continued to sink.

"I'll get back to you with funeral arrangements as soon as I get them," Logan said.

"Thanks." Randall ended the call and stared at his computer. Brian was married and had two boys. *"Wow."*

This was too much. Seeing a man alive one moment and dead by the ten o'clock news, and now, two days later, his buddy was gone. Randall made calls to his parents and sisters. Their families had known each other for years. They were as shocked as him. Tally had met Brian once, but he didn't want to talk to her, as if she *would* speak to him. Let Omega tell her.

A sober mood engulfed Randall for the rest of the day. Logan had texted him with the details for the wake and funeral. The family had also requested a fraternity memorial at the visitation.

It had been a long time since Randall donned the red blazer, white shirt, black pants, and red tie to perform the scripted ritual.

A few evenings later, twelve Kappas entered the funeral home two by two an hour into the family visitation at the wake. Randall would have thought it would have been more, but sometimes death didn't interrupt other people's plans.

Lining in front of Brian's black casket, the frat brothers sang the Kappa hymn, then the chapter president read the proclamation.

"Although Brian's accomplishments in education and the community were endless, he remained active in our chapter." Zane Carter said he served as treasurer, then listed all the non-organizations that had benefited from his generosity.

Randall already knew most of what Zane said, except for his recent volunteerism with his wife at a church pantry.

Zane gave the framed proclamation to his wife with the fraternity's commitment to be at her beck-and-call for anything with their condolences.

The following day for the funeral, Randall and Logan greeted more fraternity brothers who hadn't attended the wake.

Randall scanned the order of service on the program. There was a soloist, Scriptures, designated speakers to give remarks, the eulogy, another song, then the parting view.

"Time and chance happen to us all," Reverend Kenneth Nelson began. "We don't know when the end will come. Brian suffered a massive heart attack. A week prior, he told his wife that he felt Jesus was coming for him out of the blue. Brian repented the next day and found a church to baptize him in Jesus' name to wash away his sins. Praise God. It's never too late to come to God as long as you are alive."

What did Brian mean he felt that Jesus was coming for him? Randall wondered. Brian was a good guy, husband, and father. Why would the Lord take him so soon? Randall wasn't convinced of the story the preacher presented.

The minister continued, "I stand here today knowing little about Brian's past, but I have a glimpse of his eternal future with Jesus. The last shall be first, and the first last. No one can beat us to heaven, but it is a race to get there. Brian didn't lose."

"Amen," Randall felt obligated to mumble along with the others.

Brian's early death taught Randall one thing. To check in with his friends more often.

After the parting view, Randall gathered outside to catch up with some of his frat brothers who weren't designated pallbearers before getting into their cars for the funeral possession to the cemetery. As Randall turned to leave, a familiar face came into view—the Jude dude.

He hoped the man didn't see him. Just his luck. They had parked next to each other.

"Randall, right?" The minister held out his hand for a shake.

He accepted. "How do you know Brian?"

"He lived next door to my family when we were children, and his wife is a distant cousin." Jude's voice had a somber tone. "Funerals make us think about our mortality, don't they? Every time I attend one, I wonder what others will think about my life and if it matches what God has written about me in His Book of Life. Brian got the chance to repent and get his sins washed away. Have you?"

What was this man insinuating? That struck a nerve with Randall.

Jude didn't give him a chance to answer. "If you decide to visit Christ For All again, besides your sister and brother-in-law, I'd be glad to see you, brother."

"Yeah." This was too much church in one day. Randall had already heard a eulogy. He didn't need Jude to add a footnote too. Randall slipped into his car and hung the tag for other motorists to see he was part of the mourners.

Randall steered his car into position behind another vehicle in the procession. His mind rewound to part of the eulogy—the first shall be last, and the last first. Maybe, one day, he'd get first at the back of the line.

Not today.

Chapter Thirteen

But my God shall supply all your needs according to his riches
in glory by Christ Jesus. —Philippians 4:19

S inclaire was learning to expect the unexpected regarding the
Lord's will. The unexpected call from an unexpected person
had Sinclaire on the verge of tears.

"Tally mentioned that you were job hunting. Are you
interested in part-time work?" Sister Omega Franklin asked.

"Yes," Sinclaire answered. It would supplement the income
during gaps from her contract projects.

Her friend was incredible. Even though Tally had been out
of work, she treated Sinclaire and her family to Sunday dinners
when she dropped Carlton off; she had the ministers open the
church to baptize her, and now she was helping Sinclaire earn
more income. The woman knew how to get her prayers
answered. Sinclaire wanted that type of prayer life.

"Great," Sister Omega said. "Let me tell you a little about
the company. Hathaway Health Management coordinates
transportation for low-income families and seniors to their doctor
appointments. Even though it's part-time, the position comes
with benefits."

"Wow." Being part of the body of Christ had its benefits.

"Tally also said you've worked remotely creating web
content. If you have a portfolio, I would like to see it, and I could
forward it to our graphics department. We had an employee who

passed away last year, and someone else has been on double duty since... never mind the details. We have a vacancy."

"Thank you for thinking of me, and I'll have to thank Tally. I'm going to miss her blessing me in ways I never thought."

"You have no idea how much my family will miss her too. She's been like a big sister to me and Delta with her petite self."

"I'll get that to you before the end of the day. And thank you again, Sister Omega. I appreciate everyone looking out for my family and me."

"We're all part of God's body, and that's what we're supposed to do." Omega gave her email address and her personal number. They were about to end the call when Omega said, "Oh, Sister Sinclaire, if you stay faithful to God, all those barriers from the past will crumble in the future. I'm not sure what that means, but God told me to tell you, so I guess you know what the Lord is promising you."

Sinclaire swallowed back tears after they ended the call. Her barriers to happiness had seemed part of her life, and those obstacles became bigger after each child was born. But she had done something about that thanks to Tally's urging. "Can't think about that now. I've got a job—maybe." She grinned and rocked in her chair at the desk as a new project dropped in her email.

After surrendering to the Lord, Sinclaire no longer had those traumatizing nightmares. She had been building her faith by praying and reading her Bible.

Random passages.

Some were hard to understand. The parables were her favorite.

This morning, she read Romans eight. Sinclaire forgot the verse—*And we know that all things work together for good to those who love God and are called according to his purpose.*

Was this the Lord's purpose? Excitement wrapped Sinclaire in a warm embrace. Before she could call Tally and thank her for the referral, Tally called her.

"I know you're going to apply for the job at Omega's company, right?" Tally said in a teasing tone.

Sinclaire giggled. "You know I am. Thank you for all you've done since that day in the grocery store."

"Can't take credit for that. God spoke to me and said to help you. I thought it was for groceries, but God had a bigger plan."

"Yep." Sinclaire stood from the desk in the nook she used for her at-home office. She stretched and walked into the kitchen to prepare lunch for Sissy and TJ. "Are you excited about the big move?" Sinclaire pouted like TJ when he didn't get his way. She was happy and sad at the same time. "I wish you had found something here so we could still do things together. I know Carlton is upset to see you go."

"Yeah, I know." Tally sighed. "This is life-changing for me too. I'm leaving everything behind—and everyone who matters to me—but I know this move is God's will."

Why did God's will make Sinclaire sad? She didn't voice her thoughts, and they chatted for a few more minutes before saying they would see each other at church.

Hours later, when she picked up Carlton from school, Sinclaire watched with curiosity at her son's ever-growing number of friends. They had been steadily increasing since his classmates brought weapons to school. About five boys and a group of girls walked him to her car and waved goodbye.

"Hi, Mom." Carlton climbed into the front seat and clicked his seatbelt.

"Hey, son. What's going on? I thought you didn't have that many friends."

"That was before the angels came to school with me and protected us from getting hurt. Some in my class started praying for Jesus to protect them. Thomas and Sanay talked their parents into going to church."

"Praise the Lord!" Sinclaire held her hand for a high five, then she had to do the same with the children in the backseat.

Carlton's grin was wide, showing a permanent tooth growing crooked. Sinclaire wasn't going to worry about dental costs. The Lord would make a way. "Amen."

"Mom, do you think my dad has surrendered to Jesus?" Carlton asked during the ride home.

Sinclaire wasn't expecting that question. *Hmmmph.* God was probably spanking the man now to step up. Carlton's father had been a barrier, keeping Sinclaire and her family from doing better.

Be faithful to Me, and I will crumble those barriers from your past, God whispered.

Confirmation of what Omega had spoken earlier.

While Carlton waited for his answer, Sinclaire had hers. She had started the process to get child support.

She shrugged and glanced at him. "I don't know, son."

"I'm going to pray for him." Carlton jutted his chin with determination, creasing his brows.

You do that. Sinclaire smiled and looked ahead. *Look out, Harrison. Your son is coming for ya, in Jesus' name.*

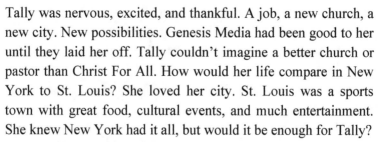

Tally was nervous, excited, and thankful. A job, a new church, a new city. New possibilities. Genesis Media had been good to her until they laid her off. Tally couldn't imagine a better church or pastor than Christ For All. How would her life compare in New York to St. Louis? She loved her city. St. Louis was a sports town with great food, cultural events, and much entertainment. She knew New York had it all, but would it be enough for Tally?

No, this wasn't the time to second-guess God's blessings.

Mother Kincaid rejoiced with Tally and shared a bittersweet moment. "I'm going to miss you the most, my mighty prayer warrior, because you've witnessed to many people and led them to Christ."

Tally smiled as she glanced at the numerous boxes she had packed. This was making it so real. She blinked to focus on what Mother Kincaid said.

Yes, Tally had been busy working for Christ—a neighbor, client, stranger, and some old friends—they had been easy. Randall had to be the stubbornest one to date.

"I guess God has some mighty work for me to do in New York City besides the new job."

"Amen. You're ready. Otherwise, God wouldn't be sending you."

"Yep. Trying to spend as much time as I can with everyone before I leave. Sinclaire and I are taking the children to the City Museum downtown on Saturday."

Mother Kincaid chuckled. "She is such a sweet woman, and her children are well-mannered. She's in the right place. We'll help her with them babies. You know anything about the children's father?"

"Nothing." Sinclaire had said there were two, but Tally wouldn't share that. "Hopefully, the brothers will embrace Carlton. Minister Morgan goes out of his way to encourage him at church."

"Good."

"Plus, you never know who you'll meet to walk with you on the spiritual journey. I'm surprised Minister Morgan hasn't tried to stop you with a proposal or professing his love." Mother Kincaid chuckled.

"*Ha!* I believe this is God's plan, I don't think Minister Morgan is a part of it right now. Don't get me wrong, I like him—his personality, looks, and sincerity with God—but he's not the one I want to wake up with in the morning wearing his ring."

"I'm glad you added the ring part, Sister Tally." She laughed.

Mother Kincaid had no idea what the Lord had delivered Tally from, but she wasn't returning to her "vomit" as the Bible mentioned in Proverbs 26:11. She accepted that it was God's will that she lost her and Randall's baby.

"I have to accept that I'll be joining the single ladies pool in New York."

"The Lord is the biggest matchmaker. Don't underestimate His plan for you."

When they ended the call, Tally wondered, *What is the plan, Lord?*

Something was going on that his family wasn't telling him. Randall could sense it. He would find out sooner or later.

His HR manager tapped on his office door with paperwork in her hand.

That immediately pulled Randall out of his musings. He groaned. "Do I want to know?"

"Probably not, but you pay me to inform you—your rules." Madison stepped into his office and closed the door but didn't sit.

"This is Harrison Wakefield's third garnishment for child support."

"Again?" Randall huffed and frowned.

"I guess he got an attorney and took care of the last one. This is a new one."

Rubbing his face, Randall steadied his breath. Employees with money problems could affect their work performance. "Okay. Tell me."

"From a Sinclaire Oliver for Harrison's son, Carlton Oliver."

"How many children does this man have?" he said aloud. "Okay. Thanks, Maddy. On your way back to your office, will you ask Harrison to see me?"

Madison nodded and backed out of his office.

While he waited for his senior analyst to come, Randall faced the window and studied the trees showing off their fall colors of gold, cranberry red, and burnt orange. He hadn't fathered any children outside of marriage. When Tally told him about losing their baby, Randall couldn't describe his mental angst. He was already in a bad mood because Tally had left him, but to know their love had created the best parts of them was devastating. He would give anything to be a father.

Harrison knocked then entered Randall's office. "Yeah, boss. You wanted to see me?" He looked clueless about the hot mess he was in.

"Yeah." Randall stroked his bare chin, a habit he picked up when he wore a beard and was annoyed. "Close the door and have a seat. I'm going to get to the point: Do you know how many children you have?"

The man looked away. His jaw moved in irritation. Randall didn't want to have this conversation either.

"Okay, here's another question perhaps you can answer. Does a Carlton Oliver ring a bell?"

Harrison exhaled. "My second son." He twisted his lips and scratched the side of his head.

Randall had met Harrison Junior. The boy was eight, respectful, and resembled his father. He never asked his employee why he didn't marry the boy's mother. That part wasn't his business. But when lifestyle intersected with livelihood, Randall stepped in.

"Listen, take care of your business. It says a lot about your character."

"Randall, I'm getting serious about somebody, and she knows about my past," he said in defense of his behavior.

"*Hmmm.* As one brother to another, get your affairs in order. Tomorrow isn't promised to us."

Harrison mumbled something and stormed out of the office as if he had been fired. The man could have a temper. Randall had seen glimpses of it when Harrison's computer designs for clients' systems malfunctioned. The man was sharp and he solved the issues, but he didn't like to make mistakes. So why didn't he keep that in mind when it came to his personal sex life?

Randall regrouped. Family was important to him. He couldn't imagine seeing his parents or sisters in need and not helping them. Thinking about family, Randall owed Delta a call. She wanted to do something—just him and her. He smiled and grabbed his phone. "Hey, sis, want to do brunch on Sunday?"

"I would but...I'm going to Tally's going away par— Ah sorry. I can't."

That wasn't a slip of Delta's tongue. She wanted him to know, yet she hadn't bothered to tell him. Randall stopped breathing. "What? She's going away. Why? When? Where is the party?"

"Chill, bro. If you had asked 'who' then you would have had the components to write a composition paper."

"I'm in no mood for jokes. Spill it, sis." Randall drummed his finger on his desk, waiting for the information. He was getting a headache. Too much stress in one day.

"You know Tally got laid off..." Delta said.

Randall nodded but didn't interrupt.

"She couldn't find anything locally, and Omega said she expanded her search. Bingo. New York came a callin'."

New York? Randall steadied his breathing.

"Anyway, she's leaving in a week. Mr. and Mrs. Gilbert asked the pastor if they could host a going-away reception at her church after their morning service. I'm not going to service, but I won't miss the party. You know, Tally's like a big sister to me."

"Yeah, I know."

"Sorry, bro. Raincheck?"

"Yeah." Randall ended the call. He was going to crash that party.

Chapter Fourteen

Now unto Him that is able to keep you from falling and present you faultless before the presence of His glory with exceeding joy. To the only wise God our Savior, be glory and majesty, dominion and power, both now and ever. Amen. —Jude 1:24–25

This was it. Tally's last time sitting in this spot at Christ For All Church. She was surrounded by so much love in this congregation. The good saints overruled insincere Christians. Then there were the Christian decoys the devil had planted in every church.

It was bittersweet. Her spiritual foundation was built inside these walls with prayer shut-ins, Bible classes, church activities, and the saints of God who encouraged her to walk with God no matter what. "Whew." She fanned herself. This was it.

"Today is the last day for Sister Tally Gilbert. She's moving to New York. Her parents are giving Sister Tally a farewell party in the banquet hall, so stop by, put a blessing in her hand, and give her a prayer of encouragement," Pastor Rodney said.

Gasps released within the sanctuary seemed deafening. Tally exhaled. Her eyes misted and her heart pounded. This was what the Lord had destined for her.

She zoned in on the pastor's message as if it were her last spiritual meal. He had referred Tally to attend the congregation at The Bridegroom Comes for her new fellowship.

"Church," Pastor Rodney began, "it's good to do a faith check routinely because the devil will chip away at it if you're not careful. How? Live Jude one, verses twenty-one through twenty-three: *'But ye, beloved, building up yourselves on your most holy faith, praying in the Holy Ghost. Keep yourselves in the love of God, looking for the mercy of our Lord Jesus Christ unto eternal life. And of some have compassion, making a difference. And others save with fear, pulling them out of the fire, hating even the garment spotted by the flesh.'"*

He stopped reading from his tablet and looked up. "This passage is a Christian's template to walk with Jesus," Pastor Rodney said and re-read it. "To be called a saint of God, check your faith every day. Add compassion and fear—not because of evil, but of losing your soul and others to hell..."

Tally listened intently. She felt like she was receiving marching orders before being dispatched to the battlefield in New York.

The intensity of the message triggered three souls to surrender, repent, and request baptism in water, in Jesus' name. One received the Holy Ghost before the benediction.

Those who didn't leave church walked to the annex for Tally's celebration send-off. Carlton held her hand as her self-appointed escort.

When Minister Morgan accepted what God had in store for Tally, he seemed to back off. She would miss his friendship.

The banquet hall was decorated with colorful balloons. Each round table was draped with a white tablecloth, which was accented with a miniature floral centerpiece. There was an endless line of well-wishers. The heartfelt hugs and words of encouragement caused tears to spill from Tally's eyes. Her mother gave her wads of tissue. Porsha stood on her left and sniffed too. Sinclaire wasn't far away, watching her other two children. Carlton remained by her side.

Of all the people Tally had shared Christ's salvation with, she was happiest that Sinclaire had surrendered and repented. The young mother had yet to see all the Lord had in store for her.

She and Omega had been working behind the scenes to help Sinclaire thrive.

Minister Morgan wasn't far away with a wicker basket to accept love offerings for Tally.

Her mother and father manned the table where finger sandwiches, cake, and punch were available. Everybody was there.

As the line thinned, Omega pulled her aside. "I'm going to miss seeing you here. But you won't be gone long."

What did she mean? Tally squinted, afraid to ask. She prayed that didn't mean she would lose her job in New York so soon. Tally had exhausted her job search locally and regionally. She had given up her townhouse and sold many of her possessions and furniture that Porsha, Omega, and Sinclaire didn't want. There was nothing left to keep her there while the opportunities in New York were endless. At least that was the story she kept telling herself.

Had the Lord Jesus shown Omega something concerning Tally? She had learned not to question Omega's spiritual gift or God's will.

"Jeremiah 29:11." Omega grinned as she and Tally recited the verse together, *"For I know the plans I have for you," declares the Lord, "plans to prosper you and not to harm you, plans to give you hope and a future."*

"Amen." Minister Morgan joined them as the crowd thinned. "Maybe this is a good time to have a group prayer."

His eyes sparkled every time he mentioned prayer as he asked everyone to gather around and join hands.

"With bowed heads and humbled hearts, let us go before the throne of God. Father, in the mighty name of Jesus, I thank You for saving Tally Gilbert. You've favored her with seeing her loved ones surrender to You. So now, we release her to You so that she can continue on the path You created for her. Dispatch Your angels to protect her. Bless her going out and her coming in. Bless her heart and her mind, and keep her safe, in Jesus' name. Amen."

"Amen," she whispered and opened her eyes. She hugged her parents, Porsha, Minister Morgan, and the newlyweds. Delta, Omega's sister, was beside herself in emotions. Tally did her best to comfort her. "Hey, you can come and visit me anytime."

"I'll book my flight." Delta sniffed.

Tally shivered. Only one person caused that familiar sensation. Holding her breath, she glanced over her shoulder for verification. Randall Addams' presence was larger than life.

His swagger was patented.

She was his prey.

It was time to say a final goodbye to her past. Randall was still unbelievably fine. His beard was gone, and he sported a mustache that was well-trimmed. He wore…she recognized the hunter green oxford shirt she had bought him. Tally sucked in her breath as memories rushed at her.

Minister Morgan stepped forward with his hand extended before she could utter a word "Randall, it's good to see you again."

"Huh?" Tally whipped her head around, severing the pull Randall had on her. "You know him?" She barely held her voice.

"I've run into him enough times to consider him an acquaintance." Minister Morgan's smile was pleasant.

Randall didn't seem to share those sentiments. "None of my acquaintances have hugged my ex."

Confusion punched Minister Morgan as he stumbled back out of the way. He looked from Randall to Tally. "Sister Tally is your ex?"

"Not my choice." Randall's nostrils flared. His fists were balled for no reason…and he smelled good.

Run! Temptation stood before her. "Randall Addams, stand down," Tally ordered. He towered over as if he was her protector. "Why are you here?" Working him out of her system hadn't been easy. She almost had a clean break, but here he was. Tally folded her arms, expecting an answer. Randall stared into her eyes, not giving her one.

"Minister Morgan, let's give them some privacy," Tally overhead Omega say as she walked him away.

The last thing Tally wanted was a scene—at church. Unfolding her arms, she placed her hand on Randall's arm.

He flexed his muscle in response. She exhaled slowly, leading him off to the side for privacy under everyone's watchful eyes.

"You," Randall said in an accusatory tone. All his emotions were raw on his face.

Attitude.

Longing.

Sadness.

"I had to see if this was true—you're leaving." The strong, brave warrior who entered the room had been reduced to a wounded animal. "I held out hope that one day we would reconcile."

She shook her head. "Me, too, but you know that can't happen without you repenting."

"I don't like to be told what to do." His silky black brows knitted together in a fierce expression while the crack in his voice betrayed him, exposing his wound.

How many times had they kissed and made up whenever either of them caused hurt feelings? Unfortunately, this couldn't be one of those times.

Be steadfast, she coaxed herself. "Which is why God resists the proud."

He twisted his full kissable lips as if he considered something. "If I did give up my will and surrender, would you marry me then?"

It was wishful thinking with too many *ifs*. Tally lifted her chin, not knowing if she was about to dare or challenge him. "In a New York minute." She grinned at her pun. He didn't, so she sobered. "However, I do believe this is God's will for me to go." Tally put up the bravest front she could while her heart was shrinking inside.

"Will you deny me a hug and kiss goodbye?"

Don't do it, flashed before her eyes like a neon sign. "A hug, but not a kiss," she told him and prepared for a long goodbye embrace. What she got was a forced hug.

Tally watched him walk away and out of her life for the last time.

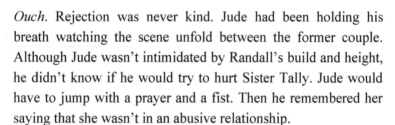

Ouch. Rejection was never kind. Jude had been holding his breath watching the scene unfold between the former couple. Although Jude wasn't intimidated by Randall's build and height, he didn't know if he would try to hurt Sister Tally. Jude would have to jump with a prayer and a fist. Then he remembered her saying that she wasn't in an abusive relationship.

Now, things made sense to Jude as he helped with the cleanup in the banquet hall. Carlton was by his side, helping the deacons pick up trash from the party. Mother Kincaid was nearby, spearheading a group to remove the decorations without destroying them for reuse.

Jude witnessed two things—love and regret. He had never been in a relationship that intense. They had a history and chose different paths. No wonder the atmosphere was eerily quiet. Tally seemed to be in her own head space, and Jude respected that.

He said his goodbyes and walked out to his car. Jude drove away, piecing together Tally's red flags, which prevented them from becoming more than friends, but in all honesty, he enjoyed their friendship.

It wasn't a coincidence Jude kept running into Randall Addams as many times as he did. God didn't have to tell him to pray for a soul when that happened. To his disappointment, Jude couldn't win Randall's stubborn soul for Christ.

Tally's hesitation about a new relationship wasn't about being uninterested or a lack of attraction. She was fighting the flesh with every bit of arsenal in her spiritual gear. He respected Tally more for her determination to live holy as God commanded for He is holy.

The Lord was drawing Randall at the same time the devil had sent a hitman to take Randall down. Did Omega's brother have a clue that the wages of sin were death? Hopefully, he wouldn't wait too late to surrender.

There was no salvation in the grave.

Chapter Fifteen

And be ye kind one to another, tenderhearted, forgiving one another,
even as God for Christ's sake hath forgiven you. —Ephesians 4:32

S inclaire left Hathaway Health almost in tears, praising God. She had gotten hired. The job gave her an excuse to leave her apartment every day for five hours. After three months, she would be eligible for medical benefits. "Yes!" She danced, standing still before getting into her vehicle.

"If you need childcare, there is a government program that will cover a certain number of hours each day," Omega had said. "Some church mothers wouldn't mind babysitting for a few hours a day too."

"Wow. I didn't expect all this kindness." Sinclaire was in awe.

"This is one of many benefits of being in the body of Christ." Omega grinned and stood. She escorted Sinclaire to human resources to complete the paperwork and take her company photo I.D.

She texted Tally. I got the job!!!!! Then added happy face emojis.

Of course, you did. Three hearts. **God is faithful in the blessing business.**

Lord, I wish Tally didn't have to go, I miss her, Sinclaire also didn't know Tally dated Sister Omega's brother. Randall Addams would have been a keeper, then she realized he didn't walk with God and Tally gave him up.

Whew! Sinclaire wanted that type of faith to turn away from temptation.

I've given you My Spirit to live right, God whispered.

Yes, the Lord delivered her from those nightmares, saved her from sin, and provided her with a steady income.

She couldn't wait to tell Carlton the good news. When she arrived at his school, a larger crowd followed him to the car along with his teacher, a short woman who could hide among the grade schoolers and no one would notice. Carlton got in the passenger seat.

Mrs. Palmer walked around to the driver's window and smiled. Her teeth were exceptionally white. "Your son is demonstrating leadership qualities in the classroom. Instead of chaos and meanness among the children, there is a degree of peace that I can't describe. I wanted to give you a good report now instead of waiting for another parent-teacher meeting." She walked away, waving at students and parents.

"I'm proud of you, son," Sinclaire said as she pulled away from the curb. "You're a role model. I know God is going to do great things for our family, in Jesus' name. Amen."

"Amen," Sissy shouted.

Later that evening, Sinclaire received a surprising phone call from a blocked number. She started not to answer but changed her mind. "Hello?"

"Sinclaire, this is Harrison." His baritone voice fell flat on her ears instead of seducing her into his bed.

"Hello. Would you like to speak with your son?" *That sounded pleasant enough,* she thought.

Carlton popped his head out of his bedroom as if he had sonic ears. "Is that Dad?" he mouthed.

"*Ahhh,* I want to talk to you first," Harrison said.

Don't be petty. "Okay." Sinclaire could spare him a few minutes. The attorney she'd consulted did say to be cordial for the children's sake.

"I can't believe you took me to court for child support." Harrison sounded annoyed. "We could have worked something out."

"I can't believe it took me this long to work it out in my head." She shrugged as she walked into her kitchen to prepare dinner.

"What about your other babies' daddies? Did you do the same to them?"

Sinclaire lifted a brow. No, he didn't ask that. First, there were two fathers, not three, but that was none of his business. What was he insinuating? "Excuse me?" She ensured her tone was sharp, so he dared not repeat his question. TJ's father had his wages garnished too. Why not be fair? Harrison didn't have to know that.

"Hold on. Your son wants to talk to you." She removed the phone from her ear so she didn't have to hear anything else Harrison had to say.

Carlton raced from his room, took the phone, then walked toward his room. "Hi, Dad. How are you? Guess what?"

Sinclaire wondered if Harrison answered any of the questions or if their son didn't give him a chance.

Tally had been right. Sinclaire should have demanded the fathers pay child support from the beginning. Maybe that might trouble their conscience to be a father to their children.

Would Harrison be honest with his son, even though he hadn't been with her?

God had shown Sinclaire red flags when she'd delivered Carlton, but she had been color-blind and in love.

"A little boy," Sinclair had cooed while admiring her baby. She looked lovingly at Harrison, who'd almost missed the delivery because of traffic at seven at night. "Let's give your firstborn your name."

Harrison shook his head. "I've always hated my name because people shorten it to Harry." He scrunched his nose. "What's your second choice, baby?"

"Carlton Harrison Wakefield."

The deer, squirrel, or animal caught in the headlights look he gave her should have been another colorful flag. He stuttered, "Give Carlton your last name so when I propose, I can change his name, too, when we become a family."

How romantic, she had thought instead of being suspicious that a proud papa would have wanted his offspring to have his first and last name. How stupid.

The proposal never came. Instead, a breakup or abandonment followed less than two years later. Angry, hurt, and devastated, Sinclaire had been glad Carlton didn't carry the loser's first or last name. Not long after that, Sinclaire learned the reason for Harrison's lie. There was already a Harrison Wakefield Jr, who was a year older than her son.

The names Sinclaire called herself upon discovery couldn't be repeated. She was a man-hater until she met Tyler, Sissy and TJ's father.

Sinclaire thought she had the right one this time with Tyler. He understood her. Adored her and Carlton. If she needed something, Tyler made it happen.

Tyler was there for her until he wasn't.

Bad habits—gambling and drinking—drew him away. Sinclaire told him to stay away from her family in his condition.

Another woman had set him straight, and they married.

Sinclaire wasn't going for strike three. She was done with dating men and the heartache from breakups. Men didn't know that she wasn't looking for a sugar daddy but a man who loved her and her ready-made family.

A man she could love and trust.

Whether that would happen, Sinclaire didn't hold out hope.

With Christ, she had clarity. The Holy Ghost gave her the power to try a person's spirit to see if they belonged to the Lord. She would not tolerate sweet-talking demons this time.

She overheard Carlton still talking as Sissy opened the bedroom door. "Dad, it's important that you repent of all the bad things you've done. I forgive you, and Mom does too. I've been praying for you because you're my dad. Don't you want to go to heaven? Jesus…"

Could she forgive Harrison and Tyler? she asked herself. There was too much damage done between her and the children's fathers.

I forgave you, God whispered.

Sinclaire stopped eavesdropping.

Why haven't you come to Me?

Huh? Randall's finger hovered over the enter button on the keyboard to sign the Adobe document.

Why haven't you come to Me?

That *was* God talking to him. Randall closed his eyes and rubbed his forehead. Today wasn't a good day for self-reflection.

He wasn't in the best of moods. His sister, Delta, hadn't been her old cheerful, sassy self either since Tally's going-away party.

Today, Tally and her family would leave or they'd left already to move her to New York City.

And so that was it.

The end of the love story his friends had envied.

Randall put his document aside and took a walk to the kitchen area down the hall from his office. His company was flourishing, and he would need to hire two more service techs soon.

God's question seemed to trail him like a shadow. Wasn't it obvious? he thought.

Pride, God whispered.

Randall couldn't argue that. It was hard to give up control over his life. He had always been a leader.

A trendsetter.

A visionary. He owned his own business because he liked making decisions and being in control. He had nothing against church, but he had to come to God on his own terms.

Wasn't religion about going to God when he was ready?

He turned into the kitchen where Harrison was the lone occupant, nursing a bottle of water with a tight grip like it was an alcoholic beverage. The man was so deep in thought that he didn't notice he wasn't alone.

Any other employee, Randall would speak and exchange light banter. Harrison was dealing with some heavy issues, so it was best to leave him alone.

Harrison glanced up. A lost expression—or maybe it was defeat—plagued his face. As if possible, his worker had aged since his meeting with Randall. He didn't resemble the man who wore his pride like a badge bigger than Randall's.

"You alright, man?" Concerned, Randall walked up to his table.

"How can I be when I've been put in my place by a seven-year-old?"

Not knowing how to respond, Randall frowned and waited for more detail.

"My son, the other one whose mother filed for garnishment," Harrison paused, "I got a little girl, too, but I relinquished my rights so her stepfather could adopt her after the first garnishment."

Ouch. Randall felt sorry for his employee's misery and lack of judgment. Although Harrison didn't ask for company, Randall grabbed the back of a nearby chair and straddled it at the table.

"I'm here if you want to talk," Randall said sincerely.

"Nah. You know my business anyway," Harrison said.

"True, but that's confidential. I won't discuss it outside my office."

Harrison was quiet, then dropped his head. Randall was about to stand, then Harrison started rambling, "Can you believe he told me to repent—he'll forgive me, and he's been praying for me?" Wrinkles cut into his forehead as he made eye contact with Randall.

"My son told me that he loved me because the Bible teaches them to love our parents, then he told me about angels protecting him at school and other church stuff that was way over my head." Harrison groaned and shook his head. "I've been reprimanded by a kid."

"Wow." What was it with all this church talk?

"He didn't ask me for money or when I was coming to visit him or give me a guilt trip about my absence in his life. He was intelligent, respectful, and passionate. His mother has done a good job without me."

Randall knew regret when he heard it. He had experienced it before. The agonizing pain was real.

"Sounds like a son you should get to know. I wouldn't want to miss out if that were me."

"Yeah. I got four women who hate me…"

Four? Randall didn't want the details, but he suspected that Harrison would have garnishments lined up.

"My mother, my sister, Junior's mother, and Carlton's mom."

At least it wasn't another mother of his child. But there were three.

Randall patted the table and stood. "Everything will work itself out."

"How?" Harrison looked at Randall as if he held the answers.

"I bet if you ask Carlton he will know." Randall blinked. Now, where did that come from? He strolled over to the refrigerator, grabbed a bottle of water, which he kept stocked, and escaped the somber mood in the room.

Omega called as Randall walked back to his office. "Hey, big brother."

He smiled for the first time all day. "Hey yourself, Mrs. Franklin."

"I love to hear people say that." She giggled.

"What's up?"

"Well, Minister Morgan asked about you and wanted me to check if you wanted to join a basketball group at church—"

"Absolutely not." And the man had the nerve to even ask.

"Why?" Omega sounded hurt.

"I don't do church, sis. Period. Now, unless you're calling to tell me you're expecting and I'm going to be an uncle or Mitchell is mistreating you, I've got to go." He also didn't want anything to do with that minister. Did he know about his history with Tally? Did she choose the minister over him?

"Jesus is calling you, bro. Pick up the phone before it's disconnected." She ended the call.

"I'm not answering," he mumbled and returned to his office. What was the world coming to? His sister wouldn't back down on getting him to church, and now his employee's son was acting like the wise parent.

Chapter Sixteen

I heard the voice of the Lord, saying, Whom shall I send, and who will go for us? Then said I, "Here am I; send me." —Isaiah 6:8

*W*ake up. There was urgency in God's whisper. *Pray.*

Jude groaned as he rolled over in his bed. He was too exhausted to open his eyes.

Someone nudged him. Living and sleeping alone, Jude was suddenly alert. He stared into the darkness except for a lone night light in the bathroom.

He spied the time. Two a.m., and he had to work in the morning. Not an excuse for an intercessor. Somebody was in trouble and needed spiritual intervention. Now! It could be a matter of life or death.

The urgency caused Jude to throw the covers back and slide out of bed and onto his knees.

"Jesus, Lord, tell me what to pray. What situation to intercede?"

Heavenly tongues filled his mouth, and Jude felt the authority and power of the Lord in the room. Someone was in serious trouble. Male, female, adult, or child, Jude didn't know, but part of James 5:16 said, *The effectual fervent prayer of a righteous man avails much.*

He prayed hard as the church did in Acts 12:5–7, and an angel of God opened the prison doors and set Peter free.

"Set the captives free now, Jesus. Freeze the bullets in the gun chamber in the name of Jesus. Let the drunk driver sober up when he passes people and cars in the name of Jesus. Give that person in the hospital hope when the doctors say there is no hope. They need a testimony. Stop the sexual assault on that child, in the name of Jesus..." When the words ran out, Jude panted for air, and his mouth was dry.

He waited for further direction as the hours passed. When there wasn't another Word from the Lord, Jude climbed back in bed. He could only hope that whatever the devil's mission was, the Lord had blocked it, so His will in heaven would be done on earth.

Randall had no plans for Friday night when Logan called him about meeting up at a club. "Aren't we too old for clubbing?" He laughed. Although bored, Randall preferred a different option.

"Not this one, bro. A new club opened in Fairview Heights. This is upscale, and some other frat brothers are going and invited us. Shower, change, and look pretty."

Kappas were known as the pretty boys to the ladies, so Randall snickered and shrugged why not. Better than sitting around watching sports. "Okay. Text me the address, and I'll meet you there."

It had been a while since he went out solo—or with a date. Randall dressed his best.

Thirty minutes later, he walked out the door. He arrived at Frederick's Night Out Club sometime later. The majestic entrance was impressive. The attire of the clientele who entered—couples and singles—was upscale.

A very pretty hostess greeted him. "Welcome to Frederick's. Would you like for me to give you a tour?"

Logan stood in the background and waved to get his attention.

"Thank you. I see my friend. I'm good." Randall swaggered to one of the cocktail tables that created a U-shape around the dance floor. A live band played an upbeat melody for its guests. The music wasn't so overly loud that conversations couldn't be had without shouting.

"The others haven't made it yet." Logan shook hands and patted Randall on the back. "How did they invite us and we beat them here?"

Randall glanced around and admired the ambiance. Low lighting. Sleek design and modest dress for their hostess. "It's all good. This is nice."

"Yeah, it's something different from hanging out at a sports bar."

They snagged a booth, and a waitress promptly brought them an electronic pad, which listed the menu choices for them to select their appetizers or light snacks.

"While you gentlemen decide, would you like a glass of wine or something stronger?"

"Stronger," Logan said and relaxed.

"Wine." Randall squinted at his friend. "I'm not going to be your designated driver."

"Chill. One drink, man, and I'm good." Logan was more than a casual drinker whenever they went out. He took any celebration—his or someone else's—to another level.

"I'm holding you to it." They ordered hot wings, dip, sliders and other finger foods to fill their bellies.

"Two ladies over there seem to want our attention." Logan saluted him and grinned, then he craned his neck and looked around. "One reminds me of Tally."

Buzzword. He made Randall look, despite knowing she was gone—from the city and his life. "Are you drunk already? No one is that fine. She's pretty but can't compete with Tally."

Logan huffed and frowned. "Why did you two break up again?"

"We," Randall pointed to his chest, "didn't break up. She left our relationship. I'm cool being single right now." *Liar.* "Yes, I lost something special, but it was Tally who forfeited a sure love because no other man will adore, treat, and pamper her the way I did—inside or outside the church." Randall was confident of that.

His friend twisted his mouth in amusement, then mocked him. "You're boastful tonight, aren't ya? I can't wait for you to eat your words." Logan winked at a woman who passed by their table.

"Enough about me." Randall stroked his chin. "What about you? You're all up in my business. I know you don't have a love life since the divorce."

"It's complicated. I have no problem dating, but I don't see myself marrying again."

Logan explained how his ex-wife, Sherry, had hired an attorney who went for blood. It was ugly because Logan's attorney retaliated. Once lovers, now they were enemies. "I love my son, but I hate that we had a child that will connect us for life. I wasn't ready for children anyway, but I do love my son." His lips curved into a smile, but his eyes betrayed his feigned happiness.

"Did I ever mention that Tally was pregnant?"

"What?" Logan bucked his eyes and leaned across the table. "No. When?"

"A year ago, but she lost it." Randall swallowed. He had become so angry at God for taking away what mattered most to him. "I'd have been a great father and husband," he said, more to himself than his friend.

When their food arrived, Randall bowed his head for his silent blessing while Logan devoured his hot wings. Their friends were still no-shows.

The band took a break and the DJ's first song drew patrons to the dance floor—couples and singles. The women who had watched them from earlier approached their table, looking for dance partners.

Logan grinned, wiped his fingers, and stood. "Let's go, pretty lady," he said and abandoned Randall.

The woman who introduced herself as Ivory slid into Logan's spot and smiled. "You don't dance?" She pouted.

"Not tonight." Randall shook his head and continued eating. He didn't want to be rude but wasn't up for casual conversation.

She didn't take the hint. "Then why are you here if you're not going to enjoy yourself?"

"Who said I wasn't? The food is superb, and the entertainment is relaxing. This is a great spot to come back with my girlfriend."

Ivory snickered. "You've got a lady, yet here you are without her," she challenged him.

"You're right. It won't happen again." He reached in his back pocket for his wallet, pulled out a couple of twenties, then stood. "Ivory, it was nice meeting you. I hope you have a good time." He walked to the dance floor where Logan showed off his skills.

"Hey, I'm heading out. No more drinks for you." Randall waggled his finger.

"Gotcha." Logan laughed and stepped closer to his dance partner.

As Randall drove across the Mississippi River to St. Louis, a sudden thought came to him: *Crash into the guardrail and see if it will hold your car from falling over.*

That's crazy. Randall glanced out the window at the dark water below. The Mighty Mississippi, known for its strong currents, seemed calm tonight.

He wasn't suicidal, so where did that thought come from? It had to be the wine, but he didn't even finish his glass.

Randall returned home without any incidents. He showered and prepared for bed. He fell asleep as soon as his head hit the pillow.

Randall's body felt drugged. He couldn't move or open his eyes, but sensed he wasn't alone. Someone or something was in his house. Where was his gun? Fearless, Randall was strong enough to take two at once if he could move, thanks to his solid muscle.

Suddenly, the darkness behind his closed eyes was peeled back as if it were a blanket, then he saw them. A large crowd around him. Who were they? What did they want? And where was he? This wasn't his room.

One man was lifted into the air, followed by a couple more, and then suddenly, thousands and thousands were caught up in the air as if they were Marvel characters ready to battle for the universe. Within seconds, they vanished, leaving him on the ground to stare after them and wonder.

Fear suffocated him like a heavy winter coat filled with bricks. Is that what weighed him down from lifting in the air to follow them? That made him afraid to be alone. Was he dead?

Randall struggled and broke free from an invisible bondage. His eyes opened. What he thought he saw wasn't real. He scooted up in bed, rubbed his head, and shivered from the sweat that covered him. Was that a nightmare? "I've never had nightmares." He couldn't recall any as a child.

He inhaled and exhaled. "What was that all about?" Randall stepped out of bed and headed to the bathroom for water. He stared at his reflection in the mirror, trying to make sense of his night after leaving the club and the dream. Somebody was playing head games with him.

"I don't have time for this," he mumbled to his reflection, then returned to bed. Sleep would not come easy this time.

Chapter Seventeen

Trust in the Lord with all thine heart; and lean not unto thine own
understanding. In all thy ways acknowledge Him, and
He shall direct thy paths. —Proverbs 3:5–6

"You're giving me a reason to follow you to New York."
Porsha would have danced in her seat if the seatbelt on
the plane didn't restrain her. "I made a list of what I want to see,
what I want to do, and where I want to shop. It's two pages."

Tally laughed. She would miss her sister's energy and spirit.
As an auditor, Porsha could live anywhere. They could be
roomies for a while until they ventured out on their own in the
Big Apple.

"Don't you dare," their mother, Cynthia, fussed from her
aisle seat on the other side of Porsha. "Who's going to take care
of us in our old age?"

"We will," Tally and Porsha said in harmony and grinned.

"Plus," Tally said, "you and Dad got some time before you
hit the big six-o."

"Still," her mother paused. "We'll miss you not being there."
Cynthia sighed and folded her hands as if she was hopeless.

"Mom, I'll be a plane ride away. I don't know what my
workload will be, but I hope to be able to come home for
Thanksgiving. I haven't missed the family dinner since I
returned from college." Tally exhaled. Her homesickness was
kicking in before the plane touched down in New York.

"If you can't, we'll book our flight to spend Thanksgiving with you." Her mother's cheerfulness didn't reach her eyes. She put on a brave front to support her girls' dreams. "And if you can't make it home for Christmas, then we'll be back."

"Not so fast, Cynthia," her father spoke up. "I'm not about to get caught up in the madness at the airport on Christmas Day with canceled flights and lost luggage."

Tally sighed. Holiday travel wouldn't be for the faint at heart, but it was worth braving it to be home for the holidays with family.

This is the path God has sent me on. She wouldn't harp on the negatives but live in the present. They had three days to explore the city until Tally had to start her new job on Tuesday at YourBrandTv.

Her mother wanted to sightsee as much as possible. Attending a Broadway play was on all of their lists. Her father, Kent, had to see Harlem and Coney Island.

Tally was excited to visit the Bridegroom Comes Church and meet her soon-to-be new church family. "You all know we're not going to be able to fit everything in one weekend." She didn't want to be exhausted the first day on the job.

"I guess that gives us a reason to come back besides checking on my older daughter," her father said, then expressed his concerns about all the stereotypes connected with New York City.

After landing at LaGuardia, the Gilberts gathered their luggage. Tally sent a group text to Mother Kincaid, Minister Morgan, and Sinclaire: **Landed.**

Praise the Lord! Mother Kincaid was the first to reply.

Amen. Thank God for traveling mercies, my friend, Minister Morgan replied next.

I'm happy you landed safely. Sad that you're gone. Carlton and we miss you so much, Sinclaire's text was bittersweet. Tally drew her to the church and felt she abandoned the Oliver family.

I miss you all too. Sinclaire, I leave you in good hands, Tally hit send.

Sister Sinclaire, we'll take care of you, sugar, Mother Kincaid texted.

Ditto, Minister Morgan responded.

Tally slipped her phone back into her purse and exited her seat when it was her family's time to exit the plane.

They navigated other passengers to follow signs to ground transportation, where a driver, courtesy of YourBrandTv, would take them to Tally's new home: an apartment in Brooklyn that she had picked virtually and paid the down payment, which was more than her parents' house note. Her things should be at a storage facility nearby.

The sights of the city wowed her family while reality set in that Tally had to adapt to this hustle-and-bustle lifestyle.

She would have to adjust to commuting on public transportation versus getting in her car and driving to her destination. Tally wasn't prepared for a compact living space at her apartment building—a third-floor one-bedroom apartment was considered spacious by New York City standards.

"It's perfect," Porsha said, trying to sound convincing but failing. Her parents exchanged skeptical looks.

"At least I don't have a roommate."

Cynthia grunted. "Where would you put her, under the bed or in the closet?"

"Believe it or not, on one website, there were pages of ads of people looking for roommates and willing to pay up to three thousand dollars." Tally shook her head, still in disbelief.

"I need to invest in property and charge rent," her father said as they waited for the storage facility to deliver Tally's belongings.

Tally shrugged. "It will do. While everything is supposed to be big in Texas, New York is big in other ways."

"I would have voted for Texas," her father mumbled.

"It's okay. I'll learn my way around."

"Do you have enough money?" Her mother gnawed on her lips.

"I'm fine. I'm a saver, not a spender, remember? Plus, the saints at church blessed me abundantly. I know how to budget, Mom, and I trust the Lord to supply all my needs."

"Right." Her mother nodded.

When Tally's things arrived, her father set up her bedroom furniture and placed her favorite blue velvet chair in the living room with her tear-drop floor lamp on the hourglass tabletop. Although she scaled back what she brought, she couldn't unpack much because of space.

Her parents would have her bed while she and Porsha would sleep on makeshift sleeping bags.

Stretched out on the floor, everyone gathered around her laptop to shop for a sofa and electronics. They ordered takeout to rest for their big day tomorrow.

"Do you think you're going to be happy here?" Her father didn't hide his concern as her mother and Porsha waited for Tally's answer.

"I'm going to give it my best." Tally didn't sound very convincing to her ears.

Her mother smiled but it didn't reach her eyes.

Lord, let this move be for my good, Tally silently prayed.

Saturday morning, the Gilberts enjoyed a tasty breakfast at a neighborhood eatery, then jumped on the subway to their destination. Riders were in their own worlds, no eye contact or smiles.

Once they made it to Times Square, the sightseeing began, then her family shopped for souvenirs. Porsha looked for one-of-a-kind clothing bargains while Tally purchased knickknacks for her new place.

The Bridegroom Comes congregation welcomed the Gilberts on Sunday like family. Despite their warmth, Tally had to stop comparing the pastor and people with those back home. That would take a while. Pastor Atkins' sermon taken from John 14: was comforting. *If I go and prepare a place for you, I will come again, and receive you unto Myself; that where I am, there ye may be also.*

"You may not be prepared for everything in life, but God has the blueprint. There are no accidents...the dots in your life do connect for God's purpose."

Afterward, they sampled ethnic dishes like Haitian cuisine before touring the 9-11 Memorial at the World Trade Center. The mood was reflective after they visited the underground museum.

Everything else on their weekend bucket list would be for another time.

That night, she swallowed back her nervousness as she and Porsha snuggled in their sleeping bags. After all, she did fast and pray for God's direction.

I will never leave you, God whispered, then caused drowsiness to descend on her.

"Porsha?" Tally whispered.

"Huh?" It was faint.

"Promise me you'll stay close with Sinclaire and her family while I'm gone. She's become like another sister to me."

"*Ummm-hmmm.*" Porsha's light snore followed. "She has a baby. I like babies."

Tally smiled and dozed off.

On her first day to report to work, Tally woke early to join the 5 a.m. prayer line, which was six a.m. in New York. She was excited to hear Sinclaire's voice on the line.

"Sister Tally, remember to fast and pray as you continue the spiritual work God began in you here in St. Louis."

"I'm saved because Tally witnessed to me," Sinclaire chimed in and made Tally smile.

"Yes, dear," Mother Kincaid said tenderly. "Be bold in your witness as you are strong in the Lord, be quick to hear, and slow to speak."

"I will, Mother Kincaid. I won't forget my foundation, and the church I'll be attending has Bible-based teaching and stresses holy living."

Fighting back her fears, it felt good to pray as she said goodbye to her family who would leave for St. Louis that afternoon. She gave them a spare key to lock up behind themselves.

Afterward, she dressed, ate, and downloaded the MTA app on her phone to double-check the train routes and schedule for delays to West 46th Street in Midtown Manhattan.

To her relief, Tally arrived at YourBrandTv on time. She had officially transitioned from radio sales to cable network sales at one of the largest cable companies in the world. Her role as manager of measurement and insight development was to ensure YourBrandTv's growth continued to branch out to attract local and regional businesses.

As the staff welcomed Tally, she wondered which person God had designated to befriend her. Everyone needed a work friend. The first day was long as she learned her job duties.

That evening, she returned to an empty space with an envelope with five one hundred dollar bills from her parents as if they hadn't given her enough as a sendoff.

She sat in her bedroom with her Bible looking out the window over the city. An occasional barking dog or loud motor disturbed her quiet meditation. "I'm here, Lord. Show me Your will."

For the first week, Tally received daily checkups from her family and Sinclaire.

"Hearing your voice on the morning prayer line doesn't count," Sinclaire said, calling back five minutes after the prayer ended.

Minister Morgan texted one time to check on her. Tally sensed the distance between them, not the physical mileage between St. Louis and Brooklyn. She felt bad for his attraction to her because she couldn't return his interest.

He saw firsthand the reason why when Randall showed up at her party. As long as certain foods, places, movies, or seeing other couples in love like Omega and Mitchell could awaken her strong feelings for Randall, it was best she didn't date anyone at her new church.

Was it a good thing Tally wasn't the only woman dining alone at neighborhood restaurants? Actually, it was sad instead of a comfort. What surprised Tally was the number of rats near the parks. She learned from a newspaper online that Brooklyn had reported a high number of sightings at untidy apartment buildings and outside restaurants to the city's 311 complaint hotline. Judging from the size of the rodents, they ate as well as Tally.

One week turned into two, then finally, Tally was adjusting to a New Yorker lifestyle. By the end of November, she should be a pro. The transition was smoother than she expected.

But for the past three days, God had laid a heavy burden on her heart to fast and pray for Randall. It wasn't the first time. *Probably not the last*, she thought. Sometimes the Lord woke her throughout the night to pray. What was going on with him now? She dared not ask Omega or Delta. Leaving for New York meant cutting ties with her past.

Chapter Eighteen

The Spirit also helps our infirmities: for we know not what we should pray for as we ought: but the Spirit itself makes intercession for us with groanings which cannot be uttered. And he that searches the hearts knows what is the mind of the Spirit, because he makes intercession for the saints according to the will of God. —Romans 8:26–27

What a difference salvation made in Sinclaire's life. Peace had replaced the chaos.

Carlton seemed to grow more powerful daily in the Lord through prayer. Sinclaire recalled how he handled a recent conversation with his father diplomatically.

"Dad, I don't want all your money. If I were old enough to work, Mom wouldn't have to ask for it. I'll save whatever you can give, but you don't have to worry about coming to play or seeing me. God is a father to the fatherless." He had quoted a Scripture he had memorized to Harrison: *He does execute the judgment of the fatherless and widow, and loves the stranger, in giving him food and raiment.* "See, Dad, Jesus will take care of me, my little sister, and my baby brother too. I've got to go now. Love you. Bye."

Sinclaire found the Scripture in Deuteronomy 10:18. What had led Carlton to find it?

How gracious of her mature son to let his immature father off the hook. Brother Mitchell, Omega's husband, and Minister Morgan took Carlton under their wings as mentors. They enjoyed sporting events or lunch on the weekends. Harrison had missed his window of opportunity to nurture and shape his son's young mind.

No sooner had Carlton ended the call than Harrison called her. She started to ignore it. She guessed it had to do with the conversation with their son.

Play nice, a voice whispered.

"Sinclaire, what are you teaching my son that he's fatherless and you're a widow? He has a father—me—and you can't be a widow if you never had a husband."

Although his anger was comical, his insult hurt, but she wouldn't take his bait. If her seven-year-old son could reign in his rejection, Sinclaire could too. "My son quoted Deuteronomy 10:18. It's three books after Genesis in the Old Testament—"

Harrison abruptly ended their connection. She chuckled. "Oh well. I was giving him the Word."

Now that Harrison was ordered to pay child support, she hoped he wouldn't disturb her peace. It didn't matter. As long as she remained cordial, Sinclaire would be guiltless.

She was about to participate in the church's winter shut the doors and pray all night service. Carlton had been ecstatic ever since Tally had told him about it. Sinclaire was curious but didn't know if she could pray that long.

Last Sunday, Pastor Rodney announced the shut-in prayer service and encouraged all members to attend. "The Bible tells us men should always pray and not faint. Pray as long as you can. The cut-off to leave would be midnight."

That's what Sinclaire planned to do. She had small ones on a bedtime schedule, so she wasn't sure how any of them would fare.

That was the plan, but that night, God changed it. Carlton prayed nonstop, and it was too late if Sinclaire wanted to go home.

The Holy Spirit had emboldened her son as he communed with the Lord in a heavenly language. Sinclaire tried to pray but listened as Carlton prophesied.

She opened her eyes to see Minister Morgan, Tally's sister Porsha, Omega, Mitchell, and Mother Kincaid surrounding Carlton, encouraging him to let Jesus use him.

How her little ones, Sissy and TJ, had slept through the noise of praise dumbfounded Sinclaire.

At three in the morning, Carlton began to lose steam and drift off.

Not Sinclaire. While she prayed, God said a man would die.

Pray for his soul to choose salvation, the Lord instructed her.

Sinclaire thought back to the day Carlton spoke to a stranger at a store who turned out to be a shoplifter. His getaway car crashed with a driver in a stolen car fleeing from the police.

Who? Do I know him? she wondered.

It was time for her to pray now that the man, whoever he was, would come to Jesus. The burden was heavy on her. Even though Sinclaire's body was weak, her spirit wouldn't let her rest as she prayed for this unidentified man.

When the shut-in service ended at seven, the saints gathered their things to leave. Porsha carried a sleepy TJ to Sinclaire's car. Mitchell had Sissy in his arms, staring at the girl as if she were his own, and Minister Morgan lifted Carlton with ease as if he weighed ten pounds instead of almost fifty.

She thanked them with a smile while her spirit continued to pray for the man about to die.

Chapter Nineteen

*Jesus said unto her, I am the resurrection, and the life: he that believes
in me, though he were dead, yet shall he live.* —John 11:25

Tally was empowered after the early morning prayer. It was
going to be a good day. The Lord would lead her to people
who needed salvation, a kind word, or prayer while bringing new
business to her company.

The evening was even better as Tally dined out at C Jazz
Club with fellow employees to celebrate her accomplishments so
far. She was settling in with a balanced life between church and
work.

Tally was not expecting a hysterical call from Omega.
"Randall was involved in a head-on collision. He's in critical
condition, and doctors don't expect him to make it." Her friend
sobbed. "Not one of my family members is saved. This is too
much."

Tally's heart pounded as she listened, keeping her
composure so as not to alarm her coworkers that she was in the
midst of a crisis.

"Jesus, please don't let him perish. Randall needs You!"
Omega's voice cracked. "I got a call from Caylee who was in the
middle of a photoshoot in London when God alerted her, and
April was on the runway in Milan last night. Both said the Lord
told them to pray for Randall. That wasn't unusual. We've all
been praying for him. God gave him so many chances to come. I
guess his time ran out."

Tally couldn't maintain her professional persona any longer as she scooted to get out of the booth where four of them were eating. "Sorry. I need to take this call." She forced herself to speak in a controlled manner when she wanted to scream in agony but kept her composure as she steadied herself on wobbly legs to walk outside.

Inhaling the cool night air in Manhattan, Tally released her own emotions. As her tears flowed, she could hear the words of Mother Kincaid, *Unbelief affects our miracles and healings.*

"Omega, we have to trust God. The doctors have given you their prognosis, but what does God say?" Tally said more to encourage herself than her friend. "It's late, but I'll go home and pack to catch the first flight out in the morning. Make sure you let Minister Morgan and the other prayer warriors know. I'm going to tell Pastor Atkins at Bridegroom Comes Church, too, so the saints here can pray."

"Thank you so much for coming and praying. Maybe your presence will help him recover."

Or hurt him more, Tally thought. "I'll be there as soon as I can." They ended the call.

I got him now, the devil seemed to snarl in her ear.

Tally growled back. "Satan, you're the master of lies, and the Lord rebuke you, in Jesus' name." With her head held high, Tally strolled back into the restaurant. "I have a family emergency at home. I'm flying out in the morning." Good thing it is a Friday, and she wouldn't miss work.

"Oh, no." Ginger, an older woman, who liked to hang out with the younger crowd, gasped. "Is everything okay?"

"It will be," Tally said with the confidence she didn't feel, but she held out hope Randall would pull through for his soul's sake and her heart's.

The intercession prayer began when she got on the train and continued to her Brooklyn apartment.

Once behind closed doors, she fell to her knees, crying, moaning, and pleading with God to let Randall live for one more chance. "Lord, have mercy on his soul. You're the God of second chances. Your mercy endures forever…"

When she no longer had the strength to pray, heavenly tongues spilled from her mouth as the presence of God filled her place.

My Will be done, God whispered.

Tally nodded and said, "Amen." She stood, sniffed, and started to pack.

Randall couldn't move his body or open his eyes. Was he having a nightmare again? Where was he? He remembered headlights in his path. Why was he in the wrong lane? Randall yelled, but nothing came out of his mouth.

He couldn't breathe.

He couldn't talk.

When Randall opened his eyes, nothing seemed familiar. He didn't recognize his surroundings. Never an outdoor enthusiast, why was he in the middle of some forest or jungle?

Insects made their presence known at the same time wild beasts snarled for their prey. He spied a tiger. Its powerful tongue was elongated ready to lick skin from Randall's bones. He shivered with fear.

Randall came eye-to-eye with a leopard. He couldn't steady his breathing. He didn't have a knife, gun, or an object to defend himself.

Time to surrender to his demise. He closed his eyes, then his sense of sound vanished. Randall spoke and heard nothing. Had he lost his hearing? There was no movement. It was like the calm before a tsunami.

Immediately, an unexpected peacefulness chased away his fear. Randall dared to open his eyes again. The thick, dark forest had been exposed to a brilliant light high in the sky. He had never seen a sun so bright it hurt to look. Randall squinted, but his eyes couldn't handle the intensity.

Yet, the animals stared at the sunlight as if in a trance.

The wind began to sway back and forth as if it rocked a newborn. The trees and plants joined in motion as if they were performing a ballet.

The birds got into formation. Not the V shape he had seen numerous times as they migrated south but in a straight line. Their wings flapped in unison.

Finally, the large and small animals rested on the ground as they waited for instructions from their Master.

The insects led a chorus with instruments—sounding like a drum, cymbal, and bass guitar.

Everything was angelic.

You would not praise Me, Randall, so every creature I made is praising Me. I am a fair and righteous Judge. God's voice seemed to walk toward him. *There I will judge you for every good and bad deed you have done on earth.* God's voice shook.

The intensity spooked Randall, but not the creatures, then he fell into a deep, dark sleep bracing for his judgment.

Chapter Twenty

That at the name of Jesus, every knee should bow, of things in heaven,
and things in earth, and things under the earth; And that every tongue
should confess that Jesus Christ is Lord, to the glory of God the Father.
—Philippians 2:10–11

The next day, time was not on Tally's side. Nothing worked in her favor. There weren't any non-stop flights until the afternoon. She had no choice but to leave her apartment at 3 a.m. to catch a 6:15 a.m. flight with a two-hour layover in Dallas. She had to get there sooner than later.

While waiting at LaGuardia, she claimed a secluded corner near her gate to pray. How many times had she prayed for someone's salvation, and Jesus honored her request? Some needed financial blessings. The Lord opened doors for them. Others needed healing from ailments. God never failed to respond. Now, here she was again, asking for a big-time favor.

"Lord, I know when I come into Your presence, You hear me because the effectual fervent prayers of a righteous man avails much. Lord, let me be righteous in Your sight." Her voice cracked. "Remove the doubt in my heart and mind to believe that You can restore Randall's health. Please let me see him alive and whole. She quoted several Scriptures on healing, including those in four instances in Matthew chapter eight, where people's faith impressed the Lord to speak His Word because it was His Will. "Let Randall's recovery be Your will, in Jesus' name. Amen."

Trusting God lifted Tally's spirit. She had released her angst gripping her, then she plummeted when the agent announced the Dallas connecting flight was delayed twenty minutes because their plane hadn't arrived. She texted Omega for updates, and her friend called.

"Nothing's changed. Randall is still critical, unconscious, and not breathing on his own. He's in God's hands." Omega exhaled, then Mitchell came on the line.

"Hey, sis. We're all here. The doctors didn't think Randall would make it through the night. He did."

Tally reached into her purse for a tissue. Closing her eyes, the tears built up as she whispered yet another prayer.

"I'll be there as soon as I can." She swallowed and ended the call. Mother Kincaid came to her mind and she yearned to hear her voice, so she called her.

"Sister Tally, I've been praying ever since the pastor made the announcement. Impress God with your faith, and pray to believe, but remember God's will always overrules ours." God's heavenly language spilled from Mother Kincaid's mouth as Tally listened. The Holy Ghost had interceded.

"Thank you." Tally sniffed.

"Remember, we don't know what's going on in the spiritual realm. We have to believe God is fighting Randall's battle for his soul."

Tally nodded, and they ended the call. It seemed like forever, but finally, Tally boarded her plane and took a window seat in the closest row to the door. After she snapped on her seatbelt, Tally glanced out the window as the baggage handlers loaded the passengers' luggage. "Lord, help my unbelief," she mumbled, reciting verses from Hebrews eleven, the faith book. She was so intense in recalling Scriptures that she developed a headache. "Lord, have mercy."

I will, God spoke to her for the first time since Tally had been praying that morning.

The Voice was audible and distinct as if someone were sitting next to her, but no one had claimed the middle seat, to Tally's relief. She wasn't in the mood for idle talk to occupy her throughout the flight.

Tally thanked God for answering. She glanced out the window again, and cloud castles caught her attention. With an unexplainable calmness, Tally smiled and admired the sky's brilliance.

One day…that glorious day, Jesus would crack these clouds and return to earth to rapture His bride—the body of Believers who had been washed in Jesus' blood. She sighed in anticipation of that hope. She couldn't wait. There would be no more sorrow or tears. Praise the Lord.

The two-hour flight seemed to drag before she glimpsed the St. Louis Gateway Arch from the air.

Yes! Almost home.

She would arrive at Lambert Airport in less than ten minutes, and Porsha and her parents would be there to drive her straight to the hospital.

Tally inhaled and exhaled to calm her nerves. She appreciated the doctors but trusted God more for Randall's healing.

The pilot came over the intercom. "Sorry, folks. There appears to be a traffic jam at our gate, so it will be a few minutes."

What? Tally groaned with disappointment. She felt faint with anxiety. The devil played mind games with her as the few minutes turned into twenty.

Philippians 4:6–7 came to mind: *Be careful for nothing; but in everything by prayer and supplication with thanksgiving let your requests be made known unto God. And the peace of God, which pass all understanding, shall keep your hearts and minds through Christ Jesus.*

Tally turned on her phone. She made calls and texts to Omega, but they went unanswered. She called Porsha for an update and got her voicemail too.

Once the cabin door was opened, Tally shot out. Fate worked against her when her gate was located in the newer terminal wing, making it a farther walk to the baggage claim and ground transportation. Being a transplant New Yorker for more than a month had its benefits. She learned to maneuver in and out of crowds to reach her destination.

As soon as Tally saw her family, fear struck. Her steps slowed until she couldn't walk anymore. Her father closed the distance.

Tears welled in her eyes. "Randall?"

"He didn't make it, sweetheart." He choked and caught her as she collapsed in his arms.

"No, no…" She shook her head. She didn't believe it.

Couldn't.

Wouldn't.

"How long ago did he pass—"

"About three hours."

She was in the air. "I want to see him. Take me to the hospital." Tally went from sorrow to mad. The devil wasn't going to win this. Nope.

Didn't she pray?

Didn't God say He would have mercy?

"He's gone, Tally." Her mother hugged her, trying to comfort her. "Randall is dead."

Shaking her head, Tally fumed. "Dad, if you don't take me, I'll get a rideshare."

"C'mon." Her mother slipped her arm through Tally's and guided her to the parking garage. "I guess seeing is believing."

While in the car, she texted Omega: **Mom and Dad told me. I'm on my way to the hospital. I have to see Randall.**

He's in the morgue, Omega texted back.

I don't care. Tell them to expect me.

Somebody lied to her, and it wasn't God. The devil was a lie.

———————◯◯———————

Tally's parents dropped her off at the hospital entrance. "We can't see him like that again. Your mother and I'd rather remember Randall the way he was."

"I'm coming with you," Porsha said and exited the car.

Linking her fingers through Tally's, the sisters kept the determined beat of Tally's ankle boots.

Omega and Mitchell stared out the glass doors, waiting for her at the main entrance.

"Tally," Omega choked, then hugged her as Porsha rubbed Tally's back.

"I prayed and prayed and prayed and asked the Lord not to take my brother." Omega swallowed and stepped back. "I never saw this coming in a vision or anything. I guess it wasn't His will." She paused. "I asked the medical examiner to bring his remains to the viewing room."

Hmmmph. "I need to be able to touch him."

"Tally," Omega and Porsha said simultaneously, then Omega continued, "he was in a bad accident. A drunk driver crossed the median. He's banged up. Swollen. Bruised. Lacerations. He's not the handsome man he once was."

"None of that matters to me." Tally fought back fear and heartache. "I want to touch his hand, rub his face before anybody else touches him. Will you deny me that, *sis*?" She emphasized the endearment because they had treated each other as such when she'd dated Randall. *I loved him so much, Lord. So much, but in the end, I love You more.*

Omega exhaled. "Okay. I'll ask."

In silence, the four took the elevator to the ground floor. The hall was wide and deserted, reminding Tally of a tunnel. The deceased bodies were brought here. Her heart pounded as she coaxed herself to be brave. She had no regrets about choosing her salvation over her love and lust for Randall. Still, she had hoped they would take the spiritual journey together. This couldn't be the end of her hope.

Porsha and Tally stayed back as Omega and Mitchell spoke with the attendant. It didn't look like they were going to win the argument.

Pray, God whispered.

Tally did, and suddenly, the attendant said, "Just this once since she came so far."

Minutes later, a white body bag was wheeled on a stainless-steel gurney. The hospital attendant unzipped the covering to reveal Randall's face. True to Omega's word, he was banged up.

Pray, God whispered.

Why? He's dead. Tally wanted to scream her frustration, but no tears were left. She glanced over her shoulder. Omega, Mitchell, and Porsha were huddled together, watching her. The attendant kept his distance to give her privacy.

Gathering strength, Tally composed herself and laid hands on Randall's cool body to pray.

"I give You thanks and praise You for Your mercy, grace, and will. Lord, in the mighty name of Jesus, You are the God of second chances. You are the God of mercy and grace."

Prophesy, God instructed. *Say what I tell you.*

Tally's heart pounded as the Lord's heavenly language filled her mouth, but she understood what she heard. "The prayers of your loved ones and saints have restored your life and those of others. I have given you more time. Open your eyes."

God breathed life back into Randall's cold body. His chest lifted. Startled, Tally couldn't move, but the attendant jumped back, shaking.

Most Bible readers knew about Jesus bringing Lazarus back to life. Now, Tally remembered how Ezekiel prophesized to dry bones.

"I am putting breath in your body. Your wounds are now healed. Sit up and worship me." Tally repeated the words God told her.

God said there would be others. Tally didn't know who they were or when it would happen, but she rejoiced for them and their families.

Randall's arms came from inside the wrapping, and he scooted into a sitting position. He began to repent, then worshipped God. Omega, Mitchell, and Porsha shouted, "Jesus," as they ran into the room and began to praise the Lord for His miracle.

Another male attendant ran into the viewing room. "Fred, you better come into the storage room. Bodies are moving in the refrigerators. Some of those corpses are alive again," the young man said with fright frozen on his face.

"What?" Fred began hyperventilating. "What's going on?" He stared at Tally for answers.

"This is God's doing. He's raising people from the dead," she explained. God brought to her mind the passage in Matthew 27:52, where tombs were opened, and bodies of the saints that had fallen asleep were raised from the dead and were seen by many. But Randall wasn't saved.

The Lord had given Randall grace because he died in his sins and escaped his judgment from hell. Her ex had a purpose. She rejoiced alongside Omega, Mitchell, and Porsha.

Fred made an urgent call with a code over the intercom to the ground floor.

That's all Tally remembered as she was caught in the spiritual realm to see angels ministering to Randall's body, touching his wounds.

More spiritual beings descended before Tally's eyes but left the room. She was clueless about why. Where were they going?

Soon, the morgue teemed with medical staff in shock and bewilderment as they examined Randall and two others in the morgue. Tally overheard them say they were children.

Yes! She would be #TeamJesus for life. Tears streamed down Tally's cheek as she witnessed Randall repeatedly repent, telling God how sorry he was and that he loved Jesus.

Although Tally had hoped to hear Randall repent, she had given up hope when she left for New York.

"Every tongue should confess that I, Jesus Christ, am Lord, to My glory that I will share with no other." God's audible voice thundered and shook the room like an earthquake.

The Spirit of the Lord was in the morgue. Tally was surprised all the dead didn't rise, but that was God's will.

Omega FaceTimed her family while Porsha did the same with their parents as medical personnel ushered them out of the viewing room to tend to Randall.

The three patients were transported to triages in the ER for evaluations, so the Gilbert and Addams family gathered at the emergency room. The Gilberts praised God while the Addamses were in shock—happy but confused.

"I want to know if my son was legally dead or not?" Mr. Addams worked himself up. "I was in his room when I thought he took his last breath. The heart monitor flatlined, and his vitals were taken. He was dead, he was dead," Randall's father repeated over and over.

There was a buzz in the emergency room as hospital administrators arrived to question the staff and run extensive tests on Randall and the children.

Randall was alive, but she could tell his soul was in worship as he barely made eye contact with her in the morgue. Finally, she could scratch his name off her prayer list.

--------------⚬⚬⚬--------------

Randall didn't know what landed him in the hospital or whether what he experienced wasn't a dream. He was alive. Randall knew without a doubt that he had heard the Voice of God.

Unbelievable. He was in awe.

God was real.

He saw angels, then doctors. As he glanced around the room, his family, Pastor Rodney from Omega's church, and friends were gathered around him. His parents were crying and laughing. He frowned.

"What happened?" he asked.

Tally stepped forward with a smile that captured his heart. "You died, Randall, but God raised you." Her eyes were swollen as she began to praise God.

Randall couldn't control his words or arms as they lifted to worship the Lord. "I died?"

A team of doctors came in with a mix of perplexity and fear on their faces. "Mr. Gilbert, I'm so sorry you experienced this, but we're going to order blood work and X-rays as a precaution to make sure your organs are operating properly." Dr. Sanders spoke for his colleagues.

"Was I dead?" he asked the doctors. His voice was weak.

"By legal definition—yes. It's a miracle you and the others are alive. The other two were in the morgue for more than a day."

Huh? Does this have anything to do with when I saw the angels? he wondered.

"It appears the others were reportedly Christians raised from the dead at three other area hospitals, two from a nursing facility, and one at a funeral home before the embalming process. It's unexplainable," the doctor said. "You were the first yesterday."

"Actually, there is an explanation. God raised them from the dead, just like in the Bible. Randall, the Lord filled you with the same Holy Spirit that He gave me, Mitchell and his family, Tally and her family," Omega explained. "Since you've repented, it's time to be baptized to complete your salvation." She clapped in praise. "Thank You, Jesus!"

Everything his sister and Tally had been saying about the need for salvation was real. Randall thought he'd experience bad dreams or nightmares, but the visions were clear as the people crowded in his room. Randall shook his head, trying to make sense of this reality. "I'm ready to surrender." He was about to throw the covers back and step out of bed when he realized he was in a gown. "Where are my clothes so I can get out of here?"

"Not so fast," another doctor said. His badge revealed he was Indian by the length of the letters in his name.

"Then I'm going to have to get baptized in the hospital," Randall demanded.

"Give us twenty-four hours for more observations," the first physician, Dr. Sanders, advised and waited for Randall's consent.

Logan rushed into the room, and his jaw dropped. "It's true." He choked back tears. "They said you were dead, and I lost it, then I got a call you were alive, I had to come to see for myself," he rambled. Logan patted his chest and exhaled. "You gave me a scare, man. So, you didn't die."

"Oh, he did," Dr. Sanders corrected Logan. "There is no way Mr. Gilbert should be here today with the injuries he suffered in the car crash."

Logan teared up and walked toward Randall's bed and hugged him then jumped back. "I didn't hurt you, did I?"

"He's fully restored," Tally said. She glowed with happiness, and now Randall understood what all the fuss was about with Jesus.

Logan turned around. "You're here, too, Tally? It's good to see you." He hugged her.

Any other time, Randall would have been jealous seeing another man hug his ex. That emotion was gone. He was glad to see Tally. Instead of the lust that was always present between them, Randall appreciated her beauty but respected her body and soul.

"I prayed. We all prayed, but it was the day *she* prayed," Omega squeezed Tally's shoulder, "that God listened."

Everyone in the room shouted, "Amen," as if they were in a church service.

The excitement drained Randall, and he closed his eyes and fell back on his pillow.

"Man, don't you dare die on me again." Logan bear-hugged him before the doctors ushered everyone out of the room so Randall could rest.

Left alone, Randall had made up his mind that if the staff didn't release him by tomorrow, he would check himself out. The sooner he could get to church, the better. He had learned his lesson the hard way. Another day was not promised to anyone, even him.

Chapter Twenty-one

"Go and tell Hezekiah: 'This is what the Lord God of your ancestor
David says: "I have heard your prayer; I have seen your tears.
Look, I will add fifteen years to your life." —Isaiah 38:5–6

The word spread. Across the city. State. Nation. The world.
St. Louis was on the map. Not about their crime stats,
but about the dead coming to life. He had seen it on television
this morning as he waited for his discharge papers.

Randall lay quietly in his hospital bed, reflecting on his life.
He saw a man get beat to death. Brian dying unexpectedly and
attending his funeral gave him pause. If God had not raised him
up, Randall would have been in a casket. The Kappa brotherhood
would have read the proclamation at his wake.

A tear slid down his face at the realization that he was a few
days to a week from being embalmed and buried. "Jesus, thank
You for mercy." God had voided his death sentence.

Someone knocked on his hospital door. "Good morning. It's
Pastor Rodney. May I visit and pray for you, Brother Gilbert?"

His mood lifted as he welcomed his visitor. "Come in."

The minister was a little man with a big smile. "How are you
feeling this morning?"

That was a loaded question where there was more than one
answer. "Like I have a reason to live."

"Praise the Lord. Yes, God is good." Pastor Rodney took a
seat in a corner chair. A black Bible was with him. He was about
to speak.

Randall blurted out. "I want to get baptized—the sooner, the better for me. I've waited long enough."

"Yes, you have." Pastor Rodney lifted his arms in the air. "Who am I to deny your request? Of course. The order of service is always subject to change." He grinned. "It's the Lord's house. He sets the priorities, so before morning service begins, one of our ministers will baptize you in Jesus' name."

An unexplainable level of excitement filled his entire being, which Randall didn't understand.

The pastor shared some Scriptures and prayed with him before leaving. "I look forward to seeing you Sunday." He left minutes before Randall's family walked into his hospital room.

Delta carried balloons and sat them on the table and kissed him. His mother hugged him then stared at him. "We stopped by your place and got you some clothes."

His father took Randall's face in both hands and kissed his forehead. Randall couldn't recall that affection happening before. "I love you, son."

"I love you back, Dad." He wrapped one arm around his father's neck and squeezed when he saw tears in his eyes.

"I wish I had been there to see you come alive again," Delta said, sitting on his hospital bed. She held his hand. Delta must have relived the moments of his demise because she sniffed.

"It's okay, baby sis. You're seeing the miracle now, I'm talking, breathing, and about to walk out of here as soon as my discharge papers come."

"I know. I believe every word in the Bible now." She exhaled. "I thought Omega and Mitchell surrendered to Christ because they almost died in the gas station holdup. I was thankful then, but now, I'm persuaded to make a drastic change too."

Randall hugged her. "I felt the same way. According to the doctors, I did die—"

"We were here. We saw for ourselves," his dad stuttered, "that our son was dead…we saw you take your last breath." Eric bowed his head as his shoulders shook. "I never want to experience that again."

Strong and fearless, Eric Addams showed Randall how to protect his family at all costs. To see his hero breaking was alarming.

His mother, who had been sitting on the opposite side of the bed, stood to rub his back. His father wiped his eyes, then exhaled. "I thank Jesus for bringing my only son back to me."

Randall had never seen death in progress like them, so he couldn't imagine their pain. "That's why I don't want to die again without Jesus."

"This has made a believer out of me. I'm right there with you, son." Eric squeezed Randall's shoulder.

"I am fully persuaded." His mother's voice was soft as she slipped her hand into his father's.

They stared at Delta.

Shaking her head, his sister looked scared. "None of this makes sense to me." She paced the floor.

"Now is not the time to copy my stubbornness. Just like Omega and Tally couldn't make me repent, I can't do that for you either. Trust me, you don't want to experience what I did." He thought about the visions—or nightmares. "You might not make it back."

"Okay, okay," Delta said.

Randall chuckled to himself. "Us having this conversation is mindboggling. I never thought I would tell God I was sorry, but I repented big time. I couldn't stop. My mouth had a mind of its own. I heard God speaking through me in a language that was foreign to my ears. Not only the language but the voice and tone." Randall was still in awe as he closed his eyes to recall that moment. "It wasn't me. A spiritual force overpowered me."

The nurse entered the room with the wheelchair. She was a tiny thing with a long blond ponytail.

"Come on, big boy." She looked at him with awe. "Time to go home and enjoy life for the second time around."

"I will."

Don't waste your second chance, God whispered. *Read about Hezekiah in 2 Kings 20.*

I won't, Lord. It was amazing Randall could hear and recognize God's voice.

"Whoever is driving can go get your car and meet us out front. I'll take him out by wheelchair," the nurse said.

Tally stepped off the elevator and walked toward them. Her strut could turn heads. Tally's smile was flirtatious without her knowing it and it melted his heart from day one.

"Hey, you." Randall couldn't help but grin. "Almost missed me. I'm being discharged."

"I'd track you down." Tally rested a hand over her heart. "I'm so glad you're surrendering to Christ." She didn't hide the love in her eyes.

"Perfect timing, sis." Omega hugged her first.

Delta was next, then his parents, before they headed toward the elevator to get their car. "You're saving the best for last," Randall said, welcoming Tally's arms around his neck for a hug.

"Okay, Mr. Miracle. Time to go." The nurse broke up the reunion as she pushed his wheelchair down the hall.

Delta and Omega were on either side of Randall, holding his hands as they did as children, trusting their big brother would take care of them. Their show of affection made him grateful for a second chance. Tally trailed them. She had been the love of his life. No wonder she wanted him to have what she'd experienced.

They stepped off the elevator to a media frenzy on the main floor in a room off the lobby area. Cameras were set up on tripods while other reporters held up their phones.

Randall spied the three doctors who had come to assess his condition sitting behind a long table draped with a white tablecloth. Microphones from various news outlets were lined up for a press conference.

A tall woman in a white sweater and black pants shouted above the noise, "Are you saying that the patients who are being treated for hyperthermia weren't dead when your hospital declared them dead?"

"Uh-oh," Delta mumbled. "We better hurry out of here before they come for you."

The nurse pushed Randall faster.

One doctor cleared his throat. "The three patients in question were pronounced dead by medical standards—no pulse, brainwaves, or heartbeat. They were transported to the hospital morgue as deceased and stored in our units at thirty-six and thirty-nine degrees Fahrenheit. Some of the patients were in there from a few hours to days."

Randall swallowed. Hearing those details again seemed unbelievable. If he hadn't been a recipient of the miracle, he would have had a hard time believing it too.

Another doctor addressed the media as the nurse was almost to the double doors, but Randall heard him say, "I'm convinced without a doubt that what happened in our morgue as well as the other reports across the city was God's doing. Some things are beyond human reasoning—"

"Can you release the names of these patients?" one reporter interrupted.

Safe, Randall thought. As his father's car pulled into the circular drive, Tally whispered, "One interview could draw more souls to Christ, so think about it."

Nope. He wasn't doing it. Randall couldn't explain what had happened to him. How could he tell others?

Media crews were among the visitors at Christ For All Church that Sunday. The seating capacity in the sanctuary was packed as a playoff game. Tally couldn't keep her tears at bay. So many emotions engulfed her. First, she never thought she would be back at her church this soon. Second, she was still processing the evidence of what she had hoped and prayed for over a year now. Randall's surrender to salvation.

Fear of losing the love of her life had tested her faith.

The joy and other emotions of seeing Randall alive again from the dead and willingly coming to church, she couldn't put into words.

Randall had boldly told Pastor Rodney when he visited him on the day of Randall's discharge that he wasn't coming to church for the sermon, but to be baptized.

Tally snickered. Some things never change. Her ex was demanding as ever, but God would use Randall's personality for His glory.

And now, Tally and the entire congregation watched the Addams family in the baptismal pool about to get their sins— visible to the eye and hidden—washed away.

When the news of what happened to Randall reached Caylee and her sister, April, they flew in to witness Omega's family being added to the Body of Christ. Tally thought about the passages in the Book of Acts where thousands were baptized in Jesus and filled with His Holy Ghost in one day.

Omega, Mitchell, Caylee, April, and Tally...the old crew were together again in the pew.

Since then, Tally's family had surrendered to the Lord and occupied another row. Sinclaire and her children were so happy to see Tally that they squeezed a tight fit next to her.

"I've missed you. We have to catch up. God is amazing." Sinclaire glowed with excitement. "Does this mean you and Omega's brother will get married?" she asked in a hushed voice.

"I hope that's on God and Randall's agenda." Tally reached for the toddler to hold. TJ wanted nothing to do with her. "Wow.

Forgotten already." She chuckled and introduced Sinclaire to the Princes. "This is Caylee and her younger sister, April. We call them our big-time models."

Tally made them blush before they chatted with Sinclaire until the moment arrived.

Minister Morgan stood in the water to baptize Randall's parents with another minister.

"My dear Brother and Sister Addams," Minister Morgan began, "upon the confession of your faith and the confidence we have in the Word of God, we now indeed baptize you in the mighty name of Jesus for the remission of your sins. For salvation is in no one else or another name under heaven given among men by which we must be saved. And you shall receive the gift of the Holy Ghost."

Mr. and Mrs. Gilbert were submerged with the thunderous roar of the church as the backdrop, then resurfaced. Both stood and gave praise to the Lord.

Randall and his sister, Delta, stepped down into the pool. With their arms folded across their chests, the minister repeated the declaration in Jesus' name.

Heavenly tongues exploded from Randall's mouth as he pumped his fist in the air.

"Yes. Praise Him," a woman shouted behind Tally.

"Hallelujah," a man sang, holding the last note.

Tally whispered, "Jesus, thank You for Your mercy and grace to make this moment a reality. You shut the devil down."

Delta began to praise God, and she, too, spoke with heavenly tongues fueled by the Holy Ghost.

Afterward, once the candidates had re-dressed, Pastor Rodney asked Randall to give his testimony.

Crossing the stage, Randall's prideful swagger was gone. His steps were confident but lacked the arrogant persona. He took the microphone and shook his head. *"Whew."* He exhaled before greeting the congregation.

Cameras flashed. The media and church members held their phones to stream live.

"Mommy, that's the man God showed me that would die when I was praying the night of the shut-in. He looks bigger," Carlton said, bouncing in place. "Wow, I'm glad he didn't die."

"He did," Tally whispered close to his ear, "but you can see that God raised him up from the dead."

"Pardon me for messing up your service," Randall said. "I had to get my sins washed away."

That brought cheers from many.

"My name is Randall Addams. Most of you already know my sister Omega and her husband, Mitchell."

Tally thought he would mention her name.

My glory I will share with no others, God whispered.

"Sorry, Lord," she mumbled to herself. It didn't matter. Nothing could take away this moment of happiness. She folded her hands and listened.

"I don't remember much about what happened, but I'll say the devil was on my tracks, trying to kill me…"

Hmmm. Tally exchanged a shrug with Omega. Both were clueless to what he meant.

"I was in a place where my spirit was left behind. It's hard to describe, but then my ex-girlfriend—"

Porsha nudged her, and Tally smiled. She would have preferred he had said her name versus the "ex" part but wasn't that how she referenced him? The "ex" word hurt and pierced her heart.

"Only thing I know is I heard the Lord's voice, and I was instantly awake. Cold. Wrapped in a body bag, I guess. I wasn't the only one raised from the dead. The doctors re-admitted us to examine our vitals." Randall turned from the left to the right. "I bare no scars today because Jesus completely healed me."

Praises were lifted across the sanctuary as Randall handed the microphone back and stepped off the pulpit. Omega stood to wave him over as many stopped him to shake his hand or pat his back.

Randall was a modern-day Lazarus. He hugged his family and hers as he found his seat.

Tally wasn't trying to steal God's glory, but it would have been nice for him to want to sit next to her instead of Omega. *I am being petty.*

She rebuked the spirit of distraction to enjoy the service. As the Spirit of God remained high throughout the sanctuary, Tally couldn't help but wonder what the plan was for her and Randall from here. She lived in New York now.

Chapter Twenty-two

Oh, that men would praise the Lord for His goodness, and for His wonderful works to the children of men! —Psalm 107:31

The media wouldn't leave Randall alone. He had testified at church and credited his sister for introducing him to salvation, and his ex-girlfriend for leaving him to force him to get his act together.

Dubbed the "Miracle 9," the media hounded all of the former deceased. The patients didn't know who had leaked their identities, but since Randall's name was out there, he gave more thought to what Tally had said about testifying for the Lord.

Right now, his passion and hunger were for reading his Bible. His eyes were opened to how his thoughts and actions offended God and his sins' consequences. Worse, the devil had brainwashed Randall not to recognize his sins as evil until he read his Bible.

He had a running list of bad deeds of which he wasn't aware.

Maybe Tally was right. Although a lot of people had heard what happened to the nine of them, there were still people who hadn't or didn't believe it. A couple whose child died of cancer and was restored to perfect health gave God the glory for the miracle. Two families threatened lawsuits for pronouncing their relatives dead when they weren't. The hospital administrators where Randall had been admitted had pushed back, stating their staff had followed standard medical procedures as the other facilities where the miracles took place.

One family was angry their loved one was resurrected because they couldn't handle a second death.

Why couldn't people accept the blessing and be grateful for a second chance?

He was. "I guess it's my turn, Lord, to tell my story."

It seemed as soon as he uttered the words, an email landed in his inbox.

I'm Kerwin Jones, a reporter with KJJX, and I would like to interview you about your experience at the hospital.

Wow. Randall rubbed his chin. "I'll do it, Lord, if you give me what to say." He hit reply to respond. After exchanging a couple of emails, Randall was set to go downtown to the station in the morning. He thought about Tally. She was the media guru, but they hadn't talked much since she was home. Randall would wing it.

The next day in the studio, he and the reporter sat in adjoining chairs facing each other.

"First of all, Randall, how are you feeling, man?" Kerwin asked. He appeared to be younger than Randall but confident. Depending on his age and where his relationship was with the Lord, Randall might consider introducing him to Delta.

Bobbing his head, Randall relaxed. He was expecting an all-in dive. He grinned. "I'm feeling good and thankful to be in the land of the living—literally."

"I hear you." Kerwin shifted in his chair. "Can you explain what happened? Were you really dead? What did you see or feel?"

"I don't think I was in this life. I can tell you that I was in a place where I don't want to go again. I felt alienated from God because things, plants, animals, and nature seemed to recognize God. I didn't, and that was frightening. I went from a dark place to light."

"Oh," Kerwin sat straighter, "so, you did see a light to a tunnel?"

"Nope." Randall shrugged.

"Oh." The reporter seemed disappointed. He exhaled. "What happened when you woke from the dead?"

Testify of Me, God whispered.

"God woke up my spirit. That's the only way I can describe it. From what I heard, the other eight were Christians, even the children, and were true Believers in Jesus." Randall paused. He wanted to get his thoughts together. "I wasn't a Believer yet, but God was merciful to me. My spirit overtook my body—my flesh—and my spirit began to repent and praise God like everything—plants, animals, the winds—in the place I found myself did. I don't know if that happened while I was unconscious or deceased, but every living thing in that place worshipped God." Randall grinned. "This time, I joined in."

He lifted his hand more than once in praise as he admonished viewers, "Don't be as stubborn as me because today and tomorrow aren't promised. I am a witness to that." He looked straight into the eye of the camera.

When the interview ended, Randall could feel God's presence as the staff congratulated him, and a few asked him to pray for them. The prayer requests surprised him.

Clueless about how to pray for others, Randall was learning how to pray for himself to please God. The repetitious phrases he heard others recite seemed meaningless to him. His prayers seemed to pour out of his soul.

Finally, he left the television station to check in at the office. This would be his first day back. Randall wanted to return to everyday life with a focus on his spiritual growth. Because of social media, he was becoming a recognizable face in drive-throughs and grocery stores.

A few days later, while Randall was in his office, his cell phone rang with an unrecognizable number. He started to let it go to voicemail but decided to answer.

"Brother Randall, this is Minister Jude Morgan. I got your number from your sister, Omega. I hope that's okay. I want us to be not only brothers in Christ but friends."

He was silent, then chuckled at his stupidity. "I thought there was something between you and my ex, and you were playing a sick game of befriending me to make me jealous."

Jude laughed. "That is way over my pay grade. When God has me cross paths with someone more than once, I know there is an assignment for me as an intercessor. I began to pray as if I knew you and prepared spiritually to battle for your soul. I had no idea that you dated Tally until at her going-away party, and it clicked when I observed your chemistry. Brother didn't stand a chance with her."

Randall's chest puffed up with that knowledge, then deflated. "Me either after she chose Christ over our relationship." That had been a painful period in his life.

"Your sister and brother-in-law never mentioned it, even when they saw my interest in Tally. I still didn't know what happened between you two until your testimony at church. By then, the Lord had revealed His purpose for me in Tally's life. It was to nourish her spiritual growth."

"Now I understand why Tally was so focused on her salvation. I can't thank her enough." Randall owed her a call. They had yet to talk in-depth because his story was in demand as he juggled endless requests. His mind wandered as Jude chatted.

News about the miracles continued to spread. Randall rarely got seven hours' worth of rest. Friends called him endlessly for prayer or to talk. His days—personal and business—had become exhaustive. Even now, his business inbox had emails from strangers. Not to mention his employees stopped by his office to check on him for a minute but wanted to hear more about his miracle.

He valued quiet time where he could meditate on God, and it became the norm for him to fall asleep reading the Bible. His soul cried out for more about the Word that sometimes it was hard to stop, regardless of the hour.

Randall realized that he had zoned out on Jude when Harrison appeared in the doorway of his office, about to knock. They hadn't talked much after that one encounter in the breakroom where his employee vented about his missteps in life after his garnishments.

Waving the man in, Randall cleared his throat. "Ah, I've got to run, but thanks for calling. We'll see each other at church. Bye." He had to consider a friendship with a man who admitted he liked Tally. To his credit, Jude acknowledged he knew nothing about his and Tally's history.

Harrison squinted at Randall. "I had to see for myself," he paused. "Madison sent the staff updates about your condition. It was crazy around here when she said you died." He whistled. "Then I saw the television interview, and you were alive. I thought she had lied."

Randall listened without interrupting. His employee seemed uncomfortable as he rambled.

"The bottom line is I'm ready to change things. Tell me how you did it. That's the only way I think my son Carlton will respect me. It's strange. I haven't been a good father to him, and he doesn't hate me for it, but I've got to do better."

"That's the right decision, but how about we talk later? It may take a while, and we both have work to get done." Randall grinned.

"Right. Right." Harrison backed out of Randall's office. "Another time then."

––––––––––––––— ∞ —––––––––––––––

"Well, I guess my job is done here," Tally mumbled as she waited at the airport in St. Louis for her flight back to LaGuardia and her new life in New York. Randall was no longer on her prayer list.

Randall Addams had been the driving force behind Tally's prayers, fasting, morning prayer line, and church prayer shut-ins for more than a year. Now that God had answered, she had to move on. Tally extended her stay in St. Louis, hoping Randall would have wanted some one-on-one time with her to share his private thoughts, which the media wasn't privy to. Never happened.

Thanksgiving with her family turned out to be low-key compared to the buzz about God's miracles. She grabbed her phone to re-read Randall's text: **Thank you, Tally, for never giving up on me. I will be forever grateful to you for pressing me toward my salvation.**

Tally hadn't replied right away. As many times as Randall hinted he would propose, now that they both were spiritually in sync, there was no mention of their happily ever after.

A part of her was disappointed that she no longer had a purpose in Randall's life. *Rejoice with those who rejoice; weep with those who weep*, Romans 12:15. Tally had already done the weeping part with the Addamses when Randall died, so now, she had to rejoice with Randall. *It's not about you!* she chided herself.

When she shared her thoughts with Porsha, her sister suggested giving Randall space to adjust to his walk with Christ.

Maybe it wasn't God's will for her and Randall to be together. Wasn't that why the Lord had sent her to New York?

It was time to board her flight. Her new life was back in New York now. She loved her job and liked her new church. That had to be enough.

Chapter Twenty-three

I am the LORD: that is my name:
and my glory will I not give to another... —Isaiah 42:8

The Lord had a purpose for everyone and everything. Tally had watched more of Randall's interviews on social media where he gave God the glory for raising him from the dead.

His fire for God reminded her of Minister Morgan. Yet, despite his package, Tally never connected with him. Would she connect with the new Randall?

Randall was a new person, with Christ taking the lead in his life. It was hard to believe he was the same person who gave his sister and Tally a hard time.

One female commentator from a cable network asked, "Did you see a bright light or tunnel?"

"No." Randall gritted his teeth. He became more irritated each time he was asked that same question.

Good for him. The world created false narratives about death and heaven, rarely mentioning hell.

"The Bible is true," Randall said. "Ecclesiastes nine, verse five says, '*For the living know that they will die, but the dead know nothing. They have no further reward because their memory is forgotten.* I praise God He gave me another chance to surrender, because the other option was dying in my sins."

There were other taped interviews about the Miracle 9 on YouTube. Thirteen, to be exact. She couldn't escape the buzz in the office when she returned to work or the misinformation she overheard on the train ride or while dining alone at a restaurant.

Hearing Carlton's excitement about school, friends, or church made her smile whenever she spoke with Sinclaire. Tally sensed her friend wanted to ask about her and Randall. Tally appreciated that Sinclaire never did.

Tally admired the wisdom Jesus had bestowed on Randall. Now and then, her name would come up in his testimonies. She was not seeking fame but the reassurance that her presence hadn't faded from his life.

New Yorkers made Christmas festive as she had seen many times on television. Excitement was in the air. Tally couldn't return home for Christmas because she had already taken days off she hadn't accumulated before Thanksgiving, so her family came to New York as promised.

They brought "home" with them with their hugs and laughter. More sightseeing was on their lists, and entertainment, including being wowed by the Rockettes in the Radio City Christmas Spectacular.

Kent Gilbert was the designated bag holder as he escorted the women down Fifth Avenue. Porsha and Tally shopped for items to bless Sinclaire's children.

Tally wouldn't label Porsha as her spy, but she updated her on how Randall was faring at Christ For All Church.

"No other sister has snagged his attention if that's what you're asking by not asking. He is really charged up with his testimony." Porsha shrugged. "I guess death is what it took for Randall to come to Jesus."

"Yeah, I guess." Tally sighed. "I imagined we'd have Bible studies together like Omega and Mitchell, go to church—"

"Sis, you're not there anymore, remember?" Porsha sifted through the bin of scarves and gloves, then moved to the table with the handbags.

"I know." Tally followed her sister after snagging a round-shaped red handbag to purchase. "Sometimes, I get caught up in my musings. Blame it on homesickness." She grinned to mask her loneliness. Tally couldn't understand her concern about why Randall's social life mattered now that he had surrendered to Christ, She hadn't dwelled on that when she broke it off with him.

"Surprisingly, he and Minister Morgan have become friends," Porsha said. "You know Minister Morgan has a habit of forcing himself into people's lives in a good way."

"He's a good guy. Randall is in good hands." Tally reflected on how he had been there for her as she navigated unemployment.

"Now, enough of memory lane. We have more Christmas shopping to do in the Big Apple," Porsha demanded.

While her family was in town, Tally curbed the urge to search for more media interviews of Randall that she might have missed since the miracles continued circulating in the news.

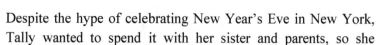

Despite the hype of celebrating New Year's Eve in New York, Tally wanted to spend it with her sister and parents, so she booked a quick trip home. Two days with family was better than being alone.

As Tally packed to be ready for her rideshare pickup to LaGuardia, she received a call from an unknown 314 area code number.

"Happy New Year." Randall's baritone voice weakened her knees.

She thought Randall had forgotten about her. It had been more than a month and no word from him. God had already chastened her about her covetous thoughts of wanting Randall to surrender for their relationship, not Him.

After she regulated her breathing, Tally found her voice. "Happy New Year to you, Brother Addams."

"Ah, the church greeting. In that case, praise the Lord, Sister Gilbert. What are you doing?"

She eyed the time. "Packing to catch my flight." *I've waited so long to hear your voice, I'd cancel the trip to talk to you, but that's not happening.*

"Where are you going?" he asked as if he had the right. She missed his caring nature toward her.

Why the petty thoughts? There wasn't any hostility between them. "I'm coming home to bring in the new year with my family." She zipped up her suitcase and checked her phone to make sure her flight was on time.

"Then I'll see you at the airport."

What? Randall ended the call before she could ask any questions. Was he coming to the airport? Excited and flustered, she unzipped her carryon and added a cute outfit. She changed from her low-key traveling clothes and put on something upscale in record time.

Her parents and Porsha didn't mention anything about not picking her up.

She applied minimum makeup. Ten minutes later, Tally's heart pounded as she stepped into her rideshare and snapped her seatbelt.

Tally didn't want to get her hopes up. Randall belonged to God now. Separating them was probably the only way they would come to Christ.

Randall's soul wouldn't spend eternity in hell but reign with God.

Mission accomplished, God whispered, and Tally smiled.

"Thank You, Jesus," she said softly.

"Excuse me, Miss. Did you say something?" the driver said as he looked at her in the rearview mirror.

"Just praising the Lord." She smiled, and he grunted.

At the airport, it was a madhouse as she cleared the security with her carryon. Once at the correct terminal, she looked for her departure gate. That's when her eyes played tricks on her.

It couldn't be.

Her eyes might deceive her, but her heart would connect with the essence of his presence anywhere.

Was Randall in New York? Was it for another media interview with the networks?

Tally slowed her steps as she observed him. The brown fedora was his signature look in the winter, highlighting his dark brown skin. In the hospital, she noticed the beard she had loved was gone. He sported a mustache only.

Moving closer, Tally noticed more. The beard was back, at least its shadow. A black-and-brown plaid scarf hung loosely over his tailor-fit cashmere overcoat. Tally was with Randall when he purchased it. He believed in neutral colors. It was either black, white, or gray. He called it brown. She had corrected him, stating it was toffee.

She smiled at the memories of their debate, which led to tasting toffee candy, ice cream, and cheesecake.

His side view was impressive. Tally exhaled.

Randall must have sensed her presence because he glanced over his shoulder and gave her a crooked smile that would end any argument. He turned and began his coordinated steps toward her. Flowers were in one hand. His other was void of an overnight bag.

His stare was magnetic, which caused Tally to freeze.

So many questions as one or two people recognized him and called his name. Randall kept coming toward her.

Lord, don't let me cry. She couldn't move.

He was within inches of towering over her. She sniffed to trap her tears and inhaled Randall's signature cologne. Gentlemen by Givenchy.

"Hi, beautiful." His eyes sparkled.

"Randall," she whispered, "why are you here?" She rambled off the question until he placed a finger on her lips, which made them tingle.

"I'll ask the question. You told me that if I asked you to marry me, you would."

Tally's heart pounded with happiness. She rested her hand on his coat where she could feel his faint heartbeat. If God hadn't raised him from the dead, she wouldn't have felt this again. "I told God I wanted a man who loved Him," she whispered. Randall was showing the world how much he loved God in every interview.

When Randall descended on one knee, Tally glanced around the busy terminal. She patted her chest to calm her nerves. It was happening.

Randall looked up and locked eyes with her in a hypnotic stare. He smiled and handed her the bouquet of red roses with sea lavender baby breaths. It was stunning.

"Thank you." She sniffed. Tally would have preferred a private moment after they had been apart, but despite being the center of attention, it felt like only the two of them.

"Tally Gilbert, you have been my queen since I met you. I realize you are my gift from God because all perfect gifts come from Him. If you still love me after my ignorance toward God, I'm asking you to be my wife." His soulful brown eyes made her breathless. "You said your answer would be yes. Is it still yes?"

A touch of fear marred his handsome features.

"I think you better say yes because I heard New Yorkers aren't friendly, and we're in their way, and I'm not getting off my knee until you do."

"I love you, Randall Gilbert. Yes." The tears fell as cheers roared around them.

He flipped open the ring box lid, which she hadn't seen in his hand. A yellow gold halo two carats diamond engagement ring rested majestically in its velvet cushion. He looked into her eyes before he took it out, slipped it on her unsteady finger, and kissed her hand.

Randall lifted her off her feet. She wrapped her arms around his neck for the sweetest kiss.

"I love you," she whispered when their lips separated.

He placed her on the ground. Randall's grin was full as he grabbed her hand and faced the onlookers. "She said yes."

Cameras flashed and videos rolled. Tally blushed and buried her face into his soft coat.

"Come on, my fiancée," Randall wrapped one arm around her waist and took her luggage in the other. His phone rang. Randall tugged her to the side to answer the FaceTime call.

"She said yes," Omega screamed.

"How did you know?" Tally laughed. She couldn't believe they were finally engaged.

"You two are blowing up on social media. A couple of people recorded it live. Congratulations." She laughed. "Trust me when I say folks got you at all angles. I guess you didn't need to buy that plane ticket for the photographer, Randall."

"Oh, yes, I did." He squeezed her hand. "I wanted my baby to know there was nowhere she could go that I wouldn't come for her." Randall winked at her. "I came to escort you back home."

"You're so over the top, big brother. Now, hurry home and bring your bride-to-be. Everyone will meet you at the airport."

Tally frowned. "Everyone?"

"Will do." Randall ended the call and tapped a kiss on her lips. "Our families and church friends, of course."

Walking hand-in-hand to their gate, Tally was full of so much emotion. Yes, every good gift and every perfect gift comes from God above. And He finally sent down the one she wanted.

———————— ⌒ ————————

Open seating was a good thing on a flight. With Tally snuggled under his arm on the airplane, Randall felt complete. He had the two most important things in life—his salvation and a woman after God's heart.

She had risked their love to follow Jesus.

He had kissed her hand more than once, which sported his engagement ring.

"Randall," she whispered.

"Yeah, baby? It's been so long since I called you that." He bit his bottom lip to relish the moment.

"Can I be honest?" she asked and continued after he nodded. "I was afraid that you had forgotten about me."

"That could never happen. Your faith in God saved me." He kissed her hair, which smelled good. Talley looked good, too, in her long turtleneck sweater, skinny jeans, and riding boots. Classy and comfortable for travel.

"How are we going to work?" Concern filled Tally's eyes. "I live in New York now. I couldn't find a job in St. Louis when I got laid off. Oh…" She brushed her nose against his. "Thank you for the money. I know you slipped it under the door."

"Yeah, I didn't like finding out about it the way I did. I've always loved you and wanted to take care of you, even if I had to do it from afar." That earned him a kiss. "You living in New York will not keep me from you. Just like I came to bring you home for New Year's after I spoke with your parents, I can visit until you move back."

"Where are you going to stay? We can't live together anymore. New York is expensive to live here, and it's more expensive to stay at the hotels…"

Amused at his fiancée's foolish talking, Randall ended her worries by kissing her into silence. He chuckled because Tally didn't say another word until they landed at Lambert airport.

"I'm so happy." She grinned as they exited the terminal.

As expected, the Addamses and Gilberts were there to greet them with balloons and signs that read congratulations. Everyone examined the rock on Tally's finger. Jude had come, too.

Porsha had brought Sinclaire. Randall didn't know her well, but he knew she was crazy about his baby, which endeared her to him. When he learned her last name was Oliver and made the connection between Carlton and Sinclaire, Randall realized his employee—Harrison was a fool to take advantage of this woman and neglect his son. His employee never followed up to talk to Randall about surrendering to the Lord.

Randall wasn't going to be the mediator between Harrison and the Olivers. He had a mess going on with three mothers of his three children. Plus, he was engaged to a different woman. Randall cleared his head to make space for Tally. They had a wedding to plan, and that was his focus.

Chapter Twenty-four

*And we know that all things work together for good to those
who love God and those who are called according to his purpose.*
—Romans 8:28

Tally and Randall had just finished their private Bible study via Zoom and exchanged air kisses. They were officially a power couple, as Tally had craved.

*Lord, You answered my prayer for Randall but separated us.
How will this work?*

As they planned for a fall wedding, Tally reluctantly re-activated her job search in St. Louis, even though she really liked her position in New York. She didn't hold back her frustration with Randall.

"The Lord will work it out, babe," he responded. Before his surrender, Tally had faith. Now, Randall's faith seemed greater than hers.

*Only by separating you from him could I draw you both to
Me for My work*, God whispered.

God's words were comforting but didn't give any foresight on what she should do, so Tally fasted for two days, and Randall joined her.

Then Tally requested a meeting with the no-nonsense V.P. of the company to discuss her engagement and the reason for her resignation. She hoped to walk away with a favorable reference.

Andrew Foss listened without interrupting. His expression gave nothing away.

When Tally finished, she waited.

"We have watched you since you came to our company. YourBrandTv doesn't want to lose your talent and vision."

That was encouraging. Tally exhaled but wasn't sure where this was going as she fumbled with her fingers waiting for him to get it over with.

"I don't see why we can't work something out where you can work remotely, but you would have to attend bimonthly meetings here in New York. That will work out for both of us."

Yes! Tally had her steps ready for a praise dance, then Andrew added, "Unfortunately," and Tally's slow grin froze, "We have guidelines in place for no transfers, promotions, or job changes until after one year of employment. That's the best I can offer, or we can accept your resignation."

"Thank you, sir, for the option. Do you mind if I talk it over with my fiancé?"

"Of course. Let us know by the end of the week." He signaled that the meeting was over when he picked up his phone to make a call.

After she left his office, Tally texted Randall. **Mr. Foss gave me options. I have to wait until my one-year work anniversary date—that's eight months away—to work remotely or quit.**

I know how much you love this position. Let's talk when you get home. Glad you have options. Your Love.

She smiled. Glad that Randall was supportive.

Later that night, once they were at their respective homes, both signed into their Zoom accounts. Randall liked to start it off with prayer.

"Tally, we will make this happen until you're eligible for remote work from here. Do I need to come every month and worship with you at Bridegroom Comes Church because you know I will?"

"And I love that about you, but since we can't live together unmarried anymore, I'd rather you not come to New York. The hotels here are very expensive. Save the money for our honeymoon to wherever you're taking me." She grinned and stared into his eyes. Sometimes they ate dinner together in front of their computers or watched a movie on YouTube. It helped them to feel connected.

Randall was quiet, then stared at her through the computer monitor. "I've always wanted to marry you."

Tally blushed as she stared at him. "I know." She threw him air kisses.

"Stop teasing me, woman. You know I can't kiss you back." He frowned, and she giggled until he gave her the option of keeping their wedding in September as they had discussed when she was home on New Year's or waiting until she moved back home in November.

"I miss you and don't want to wait any longer, but it will be hard to plan a romantic wedding when I'm so far away." She pouted.

"We don't need a wedding for it to be romantic between me and you, but if we get married while you still live in New York, I hope your bed is big enough for your husband because I'm moving there to be with my wife until I can bring her home."

Randall didn't call bluffs when it came to her, and Tally knew it. "Looks like you'll become a New Yorker for two months after we're married. I've waited long enough to marry you, and I'm not moving my date."

"Yeah. That's what I wanted to hear," Randall said. "Our parents and sisters will help with whatever you want on the ground here, baby."

"Sounds like a perfect plan, Mr. Addams. I can't wait."

Chapter Twenty-five

And whether one member suffers, all the members suffer with it;
or one member be honored, all the members rejoice with it.
—1 Corinthians 12:26

Sinclaire refused to let Harrison Wakefield make her life miserable because they shared a son.

"I've got a wedding to plan." She smiled. Would she ever be a bride? Harrison's remark, stating she had to be married to become a widow, hurt. At thirty-five years old, she was about to be a bridesmaid for the first time.

Carlton thrived at school and church with mentors Mitchell and Minister Morgan, who had told her to call him Jude, which she did.

Tally's ringtone interrupted Sinclaire's sulking, and she grinned. "Praise the Lord, sis."

She credited her friend with more than Sinclaire's salvation. Thanks to Tally, Sinclaire had an extended family at church who wanted to see her succeed. She will be with Hathaway Health for six months next week, March second. She had health and medical benefits. Plus, subsidized childcare for Sissy and TJ.

"Praise the Lord back. Busy?"

Sinclaire sighed. "Not really. Trying not to think about dealing with Harrison who is blaming me for Carlton's lack of interest in doing things with him on Harrison's court-appointed weekend custody visits. Sometimes I regret suing that man for child support."

"Don't. How's my nephew doing anyway?" Tally asked. She had unofficially adopted Sinclaire's children as her niece and nephews, and her sister Porsha did the same. Carlton loved it.

"Your nephew is excited about being in your wedding." Sinclaire giggled and stared at the invitation design she had created and emailed Tally the day before. "We all are. Thank you for letting Sissy be the flower girl, asking me to be a bridesmaid and Carlton as the ring bearer."

"Are you kidding me? No thanks needed. Weddings are a family function, and we're sisters for life."

Sinclaire loved her new life in Jesus. It came with benefits she hadn't realized.

"Let me know if you need help buying your dress or Sissy's. I gotcha," Tally said in a tone meant to be non-negotiable. "Randall insists on taking care of Carlton's tux." She paused. "Speaking of Carlton, did you know Harrison works for Randall at Tech Problems Solved?"

"What?" Sinclaire was beyond surprised. "I feel sorry for my future brother-in-law." She *tsk*ed. "I hope Randall is witnessing to him about Jesus every day. He gets so irritated with Carlton when he talks about the Lord."

"That's all he said. He didn't offer any personal conversations he had; neither did I ask."

"And Randall owns Tech Problems Solved?"

"Yes." She could hear the pride behind Tally's answer. "So, I called about the designs you sent me for the invitations and programs. You outdid yourself. Have you shown these to Omega?"

"Not yet. I wanted your opinion first." Although Omega wasn't Sinclaire's boss, she respected the workplace and was careful to limit personal projects and prayer to their break time.

"They're beautiful. You know, I was concerned about planning a wedding from afar, but everything is working out. My honey is working on his checklist, and Mother Kincaid is overseeing the decorations in the sanctuary. Hey, I have a client calling me. Talk to you later." Tally ended the call.

Sinclaire thought about what Tally had said. Randall and Harrison worked together. What were the odds of those two men crossing paths? Randall had to know about Harrison's garnishment. How was Harrison handling his boss spending more time with his son than his biological dad?

Humph. Harrison probably didn't care, so Sinclaire wouldn't either.

Months later, in mid-summer, Randall and Tally couldn't be happier as they counted down the final months before Tally would become Mrs. Addams.

The thought made him smile, but the current situation made Randall groan.

"Might as well get this over with." Randall rubbed the back of his neck and it wasn't from the day's heat. The Addams/Gilbert wedding invitations were set to be mailed this week.

"Lord, check my attitude and guide my words," Randall whispered before he emailed Harrison to come to his office.

Harrison appeared in the doorway minutes later and knocked. Randall waved him in. "Close the door and have a seat. His employee gave him a side-eye as he followed the instructions.

Since "their talk," the two maintained a respectful and cordial employee/employer relationship.

"Harrison, I wanted to give you a heads up before you receive my wedding invitation." The office was invited. Randall folded his hands and rested them on his desk.

"You need me to RSVP early or something." He chuckled but didn't see the humor.

"You have time if you do decide to attend, but your son, Carlton," Randall had to be specific, "is the ringbearer in my wedding."

Emotions washed across Harrison's face. His jaw dropped, and his eyelids blinked rapidly in disbelief. Randall could see his employee's rage building, so he braced to remain calm.

Harrison squinted as he gripped the chair's armrests, scooting to the edge. "How do you know my son?"

"Church. My fiancée and Sinclaire are good friends."

"Now everything is starting to make sense. No wonder he's busy with church." Harrison gritted his teeth. "And you're just now telling me this?"

"I put two and two together when I met her earlier this year. I'm one of Carlton's mentors. Your name never came up in an outing. I'm not trying to be a middleman between father and son. That is your relationship to build."

"Don't tell me how to be a father!" His nostrils flared. Harrison pounded his chest twice like a gorilla about to pounce on his prey.

That would be his mistake. Randall remained seated to stay calm. If Harrison crossed the line with one swing, it would take the Holy Ghost to keep Randall from responding with his own. The best option would be to have Harrison charged with assault and fired. His children would be the biggest losers because of their father's misjudgment and lose whatever financial support they were receiving.

Humph. "And here I am trying to win my son's affection, but my boss is busy sabotaging our relationship."

"That's enough, Harrison." This time, Randall stood. "I have given you more grace than you deserve—"

I gave you grace! God whispered to his spirit.

"Take a break to cool off, then go back to work. Here's a warning. Never come at me like that again, or I will terminate you." He squinted. "Do we have an understanding?"

Harrison stood without answering and left Randall's office.

Epilogue

*For the LORD God is a sun and shield: the LORD will give grace
and glory: no good thing will He withhold from them that walk
uprightly.* —Psalm 84:11

September. Six months later…

T he wedding was more romantic than Tally could have
imagined. Randall's surprises had wowed her. She felt his
love.

After exchanging vows, a horse-drawn carriage whisked
them away to their reception. Friends followed in their decorated
cars with balloons and ribbons. It was like a parade. Everything
was perfect!

The hiccup Randall didn't share was his confrontation with
Harrison when he learned Carlton was the ring bearer in their
wedding. He accused Randall of stealing his son's affection and
threatened Randall to stay away from Carlton, or he would crash
the wedding.

Praise God that Harrison didn't ruin their big day.

Randall had told him, "If you value your life and your job, I
would rethink that plan if I were you."

To make sure Harrison didn't test him, his frat brothers were
more than happy to act as security detail and bodyguards. Tally
was glad he didn't tell her any of that. She also praised Jesus that
Randall handled the situation in a Christian manner versus a
beatdown.

Randall was a strong godly man now. She had seen all sides of his emotions—happy, sad, upset, and miserable—but she had never seen him cry tears of joy as he professed his love and faithfulness.

She held his vows close to her heart.

"Tally, God planted you in my heart before I met you. I lost you, then I found you, and with God's help, I'll never let you go. I promise to be faithful and care for you in sickness and health. Even when death tried to part us, God said no. I'm hoping for a long life together."

Mr. Addams, Randall's father and the best man, handed him a handkerchief. Tally took it and patted his tears dry, mouthing, "I love you so much." Afterward, he kissed her hand.

His groomsmen: his best friend Logan, his brother-in-law Mitchell, and Minister Morgan, cleared their throats.

Porsha was Tally's maid of honor. Her bridesmaids were Omega and Sinclaire. Her vows were also heartfelt. "I'm forever grateful that God honors faithfulness. You are the man the Lord handpicked for me. I hope to show you how much I love you as I respect your decisions and be faithful until the end."

Everything else about the ceremony was a blur. After two hours of mingling at their reception, Tally and her husband slipped away for their honeymoon in Greece on the Santorini Islands.

It was day three, and all those memories remained fresh in her mind, including his proposal in the busy LaGuardia airport.

She was in awe of waking up with a rock on her finger, and Randall kissed her hand every night before they said good night.

On day ten, she and Randall boarded the plane for the States. Tally assumed they would fly back to St. Louis for a couple of days before she had to return to New York.

"What's going on?" Tally frowned at the ticket gate that wasn't for a St. Louis departure.

"I'm coming to New York with my wife, and when I leave in a few months, you're coming with me," Randall said as they boarded the plane.

Tally playfully scrunched her nose. "Whoa, my husband is full of surprises. Ah, that's why you packed more luggage than me." She wrapped her arms around his waist. "And I thought my husband was just being a divo."

"Nope. Until death do us part." He kissed her lips, then they buckled up to begin their journey, never forgetting the day she prayed for him, and the Lord answered.

Book Club Discussion

1. Share your testimony about your salvation journey.

2. Share a time when the Lord has led you to pray, and you didn't know the reason at the time, and it was later revealed.

3. Discuss how God used Carlton Oliver for ministry.

4. What role did Minister Jude Morgan play in the story?

5. Discuss Tally's internal thoughts after God delivered on her request for Randall's salvation.

6. Should Randall have told Harrison he was mentoring Carlton? Why, or why not?

7. What would you do with a second chance at life? Would you make it count spiritually?

8. Evaluate your prayer life. Healthy or need inspiration for improvement?

Author's Notes:

I count it a privilege to bring you the Intercessors stories. God tells us to pray and not faint.

In case you're wondering, there is documented proof that a young man within our organization, Pentecostal Assemblies of the World, died. His mother, Evangelist Mildred Boyd from Indianapolis, who was out of town when she received the word, returned home and prayed. God restored Otis Boyd's life. Read about the miracles God performed through her in the book, *He's the Master of Every Situation: the Life and Faith of Mother Boyd.*

Also, God used Evangelist Mattie B. Poole to perform miracles when she was alive. Read more about her on YouTube, Facebook, and here: evangelistmattiebpoole.blogspot.com

About the Author

Pat Simmons is a multi-published Christian romance author of forty-plus titles. She is a self-proclaimed genealogy sleuth who is passionate about researching her ancestors, then casting them in starring roles in her novels. She is a five-time recipient of the RSJ Emma Rodgers Award for Best Inspirational Romance: *Still Guilty, Crowning Glory, The Confession, Christmas Dinner*, and *Queen's Surrender (To A Higher Calling)*. Pat's first inspirational women's fiction, *Lean On Me*, with Sourcebooks, was the February/March Together We Read Digital Book Club pick for the national library system. *Here for You* and *Stand by Me* are also part of the Family is Forever series. Her holiday indie release, *Christmas Dinner*, and traditionally published, *Here for You* were featured in *Woman's World*, a national magazine. *Here for You* was also listed in the "7 Great Reads That Help to Keep the Faith" by Sisters From AARP. She contributed an article, "I'm Listening," in the *Chicken Soup for the Soul: I'm Speaking Now* (2021). Pat is the recipient of the 2022 Leslie Esdaile "Trailblazer" Award given by Building Relationships Around Books Readers' Choice for her work in the Christian fiction genre.

As a Christian, Pat describes the evidence of the gift of the Holy Ghost as a life-altering experience. She has been a featured speaker and workshop presenter at various venues across the country. Pat has converted her sofa-strapped sports fanatical husband into an amateur travel agent, untrained bodyguard, GPS-guided chauffeur, and administrative assistant who is constantly on probation. They have a son and a daughter. Pat holds a B.S. in mass communications from Emerson College in Boston, Massachusetts and has worked in radio, television, and print media for more than twenty years. She oversaw the media publicity for the annual RT Booklovers Conventions for fourteen years. Visit her at www.patsimmons.net.

Other Christian Titles

The Jamieson Legacy series
Book 1: Guilty of Love
Book 2: Not Guilty of Love
Book 3: Still Guilty
Book 4: The Acquittal
Book 5: Guilty by Association
Book 6: The Guilt Trip
Book 7: Free from Guilt
Book 8: Sandra Nicholson's Backstory
Book 9: The Confession
Book 10: The Guilty Generation
Book 11: Queen's Surrender (To a Higher Calling)
Book 122: Contempt (Grandma BB's story)

The Intercessors
Book 1: Day Not Promised
Book 2: Day She Prayed
Book 3: Days Are Coming

The Carmen Sisters
Book 1: No Easy Catch
Book 2: In Defense of Love
Book 3: Driven to Be Loved
Book 4: Redeeming Heart

Love at the Crossroads
Book 1: Stopping Traffic
Book 2: A Baby for Christmas
Book 3: The Keepsake
Book 4: What God Has for Me
Book 5: Every Woman Needs a Praying Man

Restore My Soul series
Book 1: Crowning Glory
Book 2: Jet: The Back Story
Book 3: Love Led by the Spirit

Family is Forever:
Book 1: Lean on Me
Book 2: Here For You
Book 3: Stand by Me

Making Love Work Anthology
Book 1: Love at Work
Book 2: Words of Love
Book 3: A Mother's Love

God's Gifts:
Book1: Couple by Christmas
Book 2: Prayers Answered by Christmas

Perfect Chance at Love series:
Book 1: Love by Delivery
Book 2: Late Summer Love

Single titles
Talk to Me
Her Dress
House Calls for the Holidays (short story)
Christmas Dinner
Christmas Greetings
Taye's Gift
Waiting for Christmas
House Calls for the Holidays
Anderson Brothers
Book 1: Love for the Holidays (Three novellas):
A Christian Christmas, A Christian Easter, A Christian
Father's Day
Book 2: A Woman After David's Heart (A Valentine's Day
story)
Book 3: A Noelle for Nathan

In *Crowning Glory*, Cinderella had a prince; Karyn Wallace has a King. While Karyn served four years in prison for an unthinkable crime, she embraced salvation through Crowns for Christ outreach ministry. After her release, Karyn stays strong and confident, despite the stigma society places on ex-offenders. Since Christ strengthens the underdog, Karyn refuses to sway away from the scripture, "He who the Son has set free is free indeed." Levi Tolliver, for the most part, is a practicing Christian. One contradiction is he doesn't believe in turning the other cheek. He's steadfast there is a price to pay for every sin committed, especially after the untimely death of his wife during a robbery. Then Karyn enters Levi's life. He is enthralled not only with her beauty, but her sweet spirit until he learns about her incarceration. If Levi can accept that Christ paid Karyn's debt in full, then a treasure awaits him. This is a powerful tale and reminds readers of the permanency of redemption.

Jet: The Back Story to Love Led By the Spirit, to say Jesetta "Jet" Hutchens has issues is an understatement. In Crowning Glory, Book 1 of the Restoring My Soul series, she releases a firestorm of anger with an unforgiving heart. But every hurting soul has a history. In Jet: The Back Story to Love Led by the Spirit, Jet doesn't know how to cope with the loss of her younger sister, Diane. But God sets her on the road to a spiritual recovery. To make sure she doesn't get lost, Jesus sends the handsome and single Minister Rossi Tolliver to be her guide. Psalm 147:3 says

Jesus can heal the brokenhearted and bind up their wounds. That sets the stage for Love Led by the Spirit.

In Love Led By the Spirit, Minister Rossi Tolliver is ready to settle down. Besides the outwardly attraction, he desires a woman who is sweet, humble, and loves church folks. Sounds simple enough on paper, but when he gets off his knees, praying for that special someone to come into his life, God opens his eyes to the woman who has been there all along. There is only a slight problem. Love is the farthest thing from Jesetta "Jet" Hutchens' mind. But Rossi, the man and the minister, is hard to resist. Is Jet ready to allow the Holy Spirit to lead her to love?

Love at the Crossroads

In *Stopping Traffic*, Book 1, Candace Clark has a phobia about crossing the street, and for good reason. As fate would have it, her daughter's principal assigns her to crossing guard duties as part of the school's Parent Participation program. With no choice in the matter, Candace begrudgingly accepts her stop sign and safety vest, then reports to her designated crosswalk. Once Candace is determined to overcome her fears, God opens the door for a blessing, and Royce Kavanaugh enters into her life, a firefighter built to rescue any damsel in distress. When a spark of attraction ignites, Candace and Royce soon discover there's more than one way to stop traffic.

In *A Baby For Christmas*, Book 2, yes, diamonds are a girl's best friend, but in Solae Wyatt-Palmer's case, she desires something more valuable. Captain Hershel Kavanaugh is a divorcee and the father of two adorable little boys. Solae has never been married and longs to be a mother. Although Hershel showers her with expensive gifts, his hesitation about proposing causes Solae to walk and never look back. As the holidays approach, Hershel must convince Solae that she has everything he could ever want for Christmas.

In *The Keepsake*, Book 3, Until death us do part...or until Desiree walks away. Desiree "Desi" Bishop is devastated when she finds evidence of her husband's affair. God knew she didn't get married only to one day have to stand before a judge and file for a divorce. But Desi wants out no matter how much her heart says to forgive Michael. That isn't easier said than done. She sees God's one acceptable reason for a divorce as the only opt-out clause in her marriage. Michael Bishop is a repenting man who loves his wife of three years. If only…he had paid attention to the red flags God sent to keep him from falling into the devil's snares. But Michael didn't and he had fallen. Although God had forgiven him instantly when he repented, Desi's forgiveness is moving as a snail's pace. In the end, after all the tears have been shed and forgiveness granted and received, the couple learns that some marriages are worth keeping

In *What God Has For Me*, Book 4, Halcyon Holland is leaving her live-in boyfriend, taking their daughter and the baby in her belly with her. She's tired of waiting for the ring, so she buys herself one. When her ex doesn't reconcile their relationship, Halcyon begins to second-guess whether or not she compromised her chance for a happily ever after. After all, what man in his right mind would want to deal with the community stigma of 'baby mama drama?' But Zachary Bishop has had his eye on Halcyon since the first time he saw her. Without a ring on her finger, Zachary prays that she will come to her senses and not only leave Scott, but come back to God. What one man doesn't cherish, Zach is ready to treasure. Not deterred by Halcyon's broken spirit, Zachary is on a mission to offer her a second chance at love that she can't refuse. And as far as her adorable children are concerned, Zachary's love is unconditional for a ready-made family. Halcyon will soon learn that her past circumstances won't hinder the Lord's blessings, because what God has for her, is for her…and him…and the children.

In *Every Woman Needs A Praying Man*, Book 5, first impressions can make or break a business deal and they definitely could be a relationship buster, but an ill-timed panic attack draws two strangers together. Unlike firefighters who run into danger, instincts tell businessman Tyson Graham to head the other way as fast as he can when he meets a certain damsel in distress. Days later, the same woman struts through his door for a job interview. Monica Wyatt might possess the outwardly beauty and the brains on paper, but Tyson doesn't trust her to work for his firm, or maybe he doesn't trust his heart around her.

In *Guilty of Love*, when do you know the most important decision of your life is the right one? Reaping the seeds from what she's sown; Cheney Reynolds moves into a historic neighborhood in Ferguson, Missouri, and becomes a reclusive. Her first neighbor, the incomparable Mrs. Beatrice Tilley Beacon aka Grandma BB, is an opinionated childless widow. Grandma BB is a self-proclaimed expert on topics Cheney isn't seeking advice—everything from landscaping to hip-hop dancing to romance. Then there is Parke Kokumuo Jamison VI, a direct descendant of a royal African tribe. He learned his family ancestry, African history, and lineage preservation before he could count. Unwittingly, they are drawn to each other, but it takes Christ to weave their lives into a spiritual bliss while He exonerates their past indiscretions.

In *Not Guilty*, one man, one woman, one God and one big problem. Malcolm Jamieson wasn't the man who got away, but the man God instructed Hallison Dinkins to set free. Instead of their explosive love affair leading them to the wedding altar, God diverted Hallison to the prayer altar during her first visit back to church in years. Malcolm was convinced that his woman had loss her mind to break off their engagement. Didn't Hallison know that Malcolm, a tenth generation descendant of a royal African tribe, couldn't be replaced? Once Malcolm concedes that their relationship can't be savaged, he issues Hallison his own edict, "If we're meant to be with each other, we'll find our way back. If not, that means that there's a love stronger than what we had." His words begin to haunt Hallison until she begins to regret their break up, and that's where their story begins. Someone has to retreat, and God never loses a battle.

In *Still Guilty*, Cheney Reynolds Jamieson made a choice years ago that is now shaping her future and the future of the men she loves. A botched abortion left her unable to carry a baby to term, and her husband, Parke K. Jamison VI, is expected to produce heirs. With a wife who cannot give him a child, Parke vows to find and get custody of his illegitimate son by any means necessary. Meanwhile, Cheney's twin brother, Rainey, struggles with his anger over his ex-girlfriend's actions that haunt him, and their father, Dr. Roland Reynolds, fights to keep an old secret in the past.

In *The Acquittal*, two worlds apart, but their hearts dance to the same African drum beat. On a professional level, Dr. Rainey Reynolds is a competent, highly sought-after orthodontist. Inwardly, he needs to be set free from the chaos of revelations that make him question if happiness is obtainable. To get away from the drama, Rainey is willing to leave the country under the guise of a mission trip with Dentist Without Borders. Will changing his surroundings really change him? If one woman can heal his wounds, then he will believe that there is really peace after the storm.

Ghanaian beauty Josephine Abena Yaa Amoah returns to Africa after completing her studies as an exchange student in St. Louis, Missouri. Although her heart bleeds for his peace, she knows she must step back and pray for Rainey's surrender to Christ in order for God to acquit him of his self-inflicted mental torture. In the Motherland of Ghana, Africa, Rainey not only visits the places of his ancestors, will he embrace the liberty that Christ's Blood really does set every man free.

In *Guilty By Association*, how important is a name? To the St. Louis Jamiesons who are tenth generation descendants of a royal African tribe—everything. To the Boston Jamiesons whose father never married their mother—there is no loyalty or legacy. Kidd Jamieson suffers from the "angry" male syndrome because his father was an absent in the home, but insisted his two sons carry his last name. It takes an old woman who mingles genealogy truths and Bible verses together for Kidd to realize his worth as a strong black man. He learns it's not his association with the name that identifies him, but the man he becomes that defines him.

In *The Guilt Trip*, Aaron "Ace" Jamieson is living a carefree life. He's good-looking, respectable when he's in the mood, but his weakness is women. If a woman tries to ambush him with a pregnancy, he takes off in the other direction. It's a lesson learned from his absentee father that responsibility is optional. Talise Rogers has a bright future ahead of her. She's pretty and has no problem catching a man's eye, which is exactly what she does with Ace. Trapping Ace Jamieson is the furthest thing from Talise's mind when she learns she pregnant and Ace rejects her. "I want nothing from you Ace, not even your name." And Talise meant it.

In *Free From Guilt*, it's salvation round-up time and Cameron Jamieson's name is on God's hit list. Although his brothers and cousins embraced God—thanks to the women in their lives—the two-degreed MIT graduate isn't going to let any woman take him down that path without a fight. He's satisfied with his career, social calendar, and good genes. But God uses a beautiful messenger, Gabrielle Dupree, to show him that he's in a spiritual deficit. Cameron learns the hard way that man's wisdom is like foolishness to God. For every philosophical argument he throws her way, Gabrielle exposes him to scriptures that makes him question his worldly knowledge.

In *Sandra Nicholson Backstory*, Sandra has made good and bad choices throughout the years, but the best one was to give her life to Christ when her sons were small and to rear them up in the best Christian way she knew how. That was thirty something years ago and Sandra has evolved from a young single mother of two rambunctious boys: Kidd and Ace Jamieson, to a godly woman seasoned with wisdom. Despite the challenges and trials of rearing two strong-willed personalities, Sandra maintained her sanity through the grace of God, which kept gray strands at bay. But there is something to be said about a woman's first love. Kidd and Ace Jamieson's father, Samuel Jamieson broke their mother's heart. Can Sandra recover? Her sons don't believe any man is good enough for her, especially their absentee father. Kidd doesn't deny his mother should find love again since she never married Samuel. But will she fall for a carbon copy of his father? God's love gives second chances.

In *The Confession*, Sandra Nicholson had made good and bad choices throughout the years, but the best one was to give her life to Christ when her sons were small and to rear them up in the best Christian way she knew how. That was thirty something years ago and Sandra has evolved from a young single mother of two rambunctious boys, Kidd and Ace Jamieson, to a godly woman seasoned with wisdom. Despite the challenges and trials of rearing two strong-willed personalities, Sandra maintained her sanity through the grace of God, which kept gray strands at bay.

Now, Sandra Nicholson is on the threshold of happiness, but Kidd believes no man is good enough for his mother, especially if her love interest could be a man just like his absentee father.

In *The Guilty Generation*, seventeen-year-old Kami Jamieson is so over being daddy's little girl. Now that she has captured the attention of Tango, the bad boy from her school, Kami's love for her family and God have taken a backseat to her teen crush. Although the Jamiesons have instilled godly principles in Kami since she was young, they will stop at nothing, including prayer and fasting, to protect her from falling prey to society's peer pressure. Can Kami survive her teen rebellion, or will she be guilty of dividing the next generation?

In *Queen's Surrender (To a Higher Calling)*, Opposites attract...or clash. The Jamieson saga continues with the Queen of the family in this inspirational romance. She's the mistress of flirtation but Philip is unaffected by her charm. The two enjoy a harmless banter about God's will versus Queen's, who prefers her own free-will lifestyle. Philip doesn't judge her choices—most of the time—and Queen respects his opinions—most of the time. It's perfect harmony sometimes.

Queen, the youngest sister of the Jamieson clan, wears her name as if it's a crown. She's single, sassy, and most of the time, loving her status, but she's about to strut down an unexpected spiritual path. Love takes no prisoners. When the descendants of a royal African tribe on her father's maternal side show up and show off at a family game night, Queen's vanity is kicked up a notch. The Robnetts take royalty to a new level with their own Queen.

Evangelist Philip Dupree is on the hot seat as the trial pastor at Total Surrender Church. The deadline for the congregation to officially elect him as pastor is months away. The stalemate: They want a family man to lead their flock. The board's ultimatum is enough to make him quit the ministry. But can a man of God walk away from his calling?

Can two people with different lifestyles and priorities cross paths and continue the journey as one? Who is going to be the first to surrender?

In *Fun and Games with the Jamieson Men*, The Jamieson Legacy series inspired this game book of fun activities:• Brain Teasers• Crossword Puzzles• Word Searches •Sudoku •Mazes •Coloring Pages. The Jamiesons are fictional characters that put emphasis on Black Heritage, which includes Black American History tidbits, African American genealogy, and strong Black families. Relax, grab a pencil and play along.

THE CARMEN SISTERS SERIES

In *No Easy Catch*, Book 1, Shae Carmen hasn't lost her faith in God, only the men she's come across. Shae's recent heartbreak was discovering that her boyfriend was not only married, but on the verge of reconciling with his estranged wife. Humiliated, Shae begins to second guess herself as why she didn't see the signs that he was nothing more than a devil's decoy masquerading as a devout Christian man. St. Louis Outfielder Rahn Maxwell finds himself a victim of an attempted carjacking. The Lord guides him out of harms' way by opening the gunmen's eyes to Rahn's identity. The crook instead becomes infatuated fan and asks for Rahn's autograph, and as a good will gesture, directs Rahn out of the ambush! When the news media gets wind of what happened with the baseball player, Shae's television station lands an exclusive interview. Shae and Rahn's chance meeting sets in motion a relationship where Rahn not only surrenders to Christ, but pursues Shae with a purpose to prove that good men are still out there. After letting her guard down, Shae is faced with another scandal that rocks her world. This time the stakes are higher. Not only is her heart on the line, so is her professional credibility. She and Rahn are at odds as how to handle it and friction erupts between them. Will she strike out at love again? The Lord shows Rahn that nothing happens by chance, and everything is done for Him to get the glory.

In *Defense of Love*, Book 2, lately, nothing in Garrett Nash's life has made sense. When two people close to the U.S. Marshal wrong him deeply, Garrett expects God to remove them from his life. Instead, the Lord relocates Garrett to another city to start over, as if he were the offender instead of the victim. Criminal attorney Shari Carmen is comfortable in her own skin—most of the time. Being a "dark and lovely" African-American sister has its challenges, especially when it comes to relationships. Although she's a fireball in the courtroom, she knows how to fade into the background and keep the proverbial spotlight off her personal life. But literal spotlights are a different matter altogether. While playing tenor saxophone at an anniversary party, she grabs the attention of Garrett Nash. And as God draws them closer together, He makes another request of Garrett, one to which it will prove far more difficult to say "Yes, Lord."

In *Redeeming Heart*, Book 3, Landon Thomas (In Defense of Love) brings a new definition to the word "prodigal," as in prodigal son, brother or anything else imaginable. It's a good thing that God's love covers a multitude of sins, but He isn't letting Landon off easy. His journey from riches to rags proves to be humbling and a lesson well learned. [SEP] Real Estate Agent Octavia Winston is a woman on a mission, whether it's God's or hers professionally. One thing is for certain, she's not about to compromise when it comes to a Christian mate, so why did God send a homeless man to steal her heart? [SEP] Minister Rossi Tolliver (Crowning Glory) knows how to minister to God's lost sheep and through God's redemption, the game changes for Landon and Octavia.

In *Driven to Be Loved*, Book 4, on the surface, Brecee Carmen has nothing in common with Adrian Cole. She is a pediatrician certified in trauma care; he is a transportation problem solver for a luxury car dealership (a.k.a., a car salesman). Despite their slow but steady attraction to each other, neither one of them are sure that they're compatible. To complicate matters, Brecee is the sole unattached Carmen when it seems as though everyone else around her—family and friends—are finding love, except her. Through a series of discoveries, Adrian and Brecee learn that things don't happen by coincidence. Generational forces are at work, keeping promises, protecting family members, and perhaps even drawing Adrian back to the church. For Brecee and Adrian, God has been hard at work, playing matchmaker all along the way for their paths cross at the right time and the right place.

Lean on Me, Book 1. No one should have to go it alone... Caregivers sometimes need a little TLC too.

Tabitha Knicely believes in family before everything. She may be overwhelmed caring for her beloved great-aunt, but she would never turn her back on the woman who raised her, even if Aunt Tweet's dementia is getting worse. Tabitha is sure she can do this on her own. But when Aunt Tweet ends up on her neighbor's front porch, and the man has the audacity to accuse Tabitha of elder abuse, things go from bad to awful. Marcus Whittington feels a mountain of regret at causing problems for Tabitha and her great-aunt. How was he to know the frail older woman's niece was doing the best she could? As Marcus gets to know Aunt Tweet and sees how hard Tabitha is fighting to keep everything together, he can't walk away from the pair. Particularly when helping Tabitha care for her great-aunt leads the two of them on a spiritual journey of faith and surrender.

Here For You, Book 2. Rachel Knicely's life has been on hold for six months while she takes care of her great aunt, who has Alzheimer's. Putting her aunt first was an easy decision—accepting that Aunt Tweet is nearing the end of her battle is far more difficult. Nicholas Adams's ministry is bringing comfort to those who are sick and homebound. He responds to a request for help for an ailing woman but when he meets the Knicelys, he realizes Rachel is the one who needs support the most. Nicholas is charmed by and attracted to Rachel, but then devastating news brings both a crisis of faith and roadblocks to their budding relationship that neither could have anticipated. This beautifully emotional and clean story contains a hero and heroine who are better at taking care of other people than themselves, a dark moment that shakes their faith, and a well-earned happily ever after.

Stand by Me, Book 3. An uplifting story about embracing love and giving others—and yourself—one more chance. When it comes to being a caregiver, Kym Knicely has been there and done that. Then she meets Charles "Chaz" Banks and soon learns that every caregiving situation is different. Chaz takes care of his seven-year-old autistic granddaughter, Chauncy. Although Kym's attraction to Chaz is strong, she has to decide whether a romantic relationship can survive and thrive between two people at different stages in life. It's a journey with a different set of rules that Kym has to play by if she and Chaz are to have their happily ever after and the faith and family they envision.

About *Waiting for Christmas*,

A chance meeting. An undeniable attraction.

And a first date that starts with a stakeout that leads to a winner takes all shopping spree. It's the making of a holiday romance. While philanthropist Sterling Price believes in charitable causes, he and licensed social worker Ciara Summers have a difference of opinion on how to bless others. Ciara is a rebel with a cause and a hundred reasons why helping those less fortunate is important. Sterling is a man of means who believes there is a financial responsibility that comes with giving.

The Lord will make sure everyone's needs are met, and He has something extra for Sterling and Ciara that can't wait until Christmas.

About *Christmas Dinner,*

How do you celebrate the holidays after losing a loved one? Take the journey, beginning with Christmas Dinner. For months, Darcelle Price has suffered depression in silence. But things are about to change as she plans to celebrate Christmas Eve with family and share her journey. Darcelle invites them via group text, not knowing she had included her ex. Evanston Giles is surprised to hear from the woman he loved after months following their breakup. Seeking closure, he shows up on her doorsteps for answers. A lot can happen on Christmas Eve. Restoring family ties, building her faith in God, and falling in love again are just the beginning of the night of miracles.

About *Taye's Gift*,

Welcome to Snowflake, Colorado—a small town where wishes come true! When six old high school friends receive a letter that their fellow friend, Charity Hart, wrote before she passed away, their lives take an unexpected turn. She leaves them each a check for $1,500 and asks them to grant a wish—a secret wish—for someone else by Christmas. Who lays off someone before the holidays? Taye Thomas' employer did, so instead of Christmas shopping, she's job hunting. More devastating news comes when an old high school friend passed away. Could God be answering her prayers for help when she learns that Charity Hart left a $1500 check? No, the caveat is it's more blessed to give than receive. Taye has 30 days to find someone else in need to bless. To complicate matters, she's lives in Kansas City, which is more than eight hours away from Snowflake and she can't do it alone. Keeping a secret has never been so much work.

About *Couple by Christmas*,

Holidays haven't been the same for Derek Washington since his divorce. He and his ex-wife, Robyn, go out of their way to avoid each other. This Christmas may be different when he decides to give his son, Tyler, the family he once had before they split. Derek's going to need the Lord's intervention to soften her heart to agree to some outings. God's help doesn't come in the way he expected, but it's all good because everything falls in place for them to be a couple by Christmas.

About *Prayers Answered By Christmas*,

Christmas is coming. While other children are compiling their lists for a fictional Santa, eight-year-old Mikaela Washington is on her knees, making her requests known to the Lord: One mommy for Christmas please. Portia Hunter refuses to let her ex-husband cheat her out of the family she wants. Her prayer is for God to send the right man into her life. Marlon Washington will do anything for his two little girls, but can he find a mommy for them and a love for himself? Since Christmas is the time of year to remember the many gifts God has given men, maybe these three souls will get their heart s desire.

About *A Noelle for Nathan*,

A Noelle for Nathan is a story of kindness, selflessness, and falling in love during the Christmas season. Andersen Investors & Consultants, LLC, CFO Nathan Andersen (A Christian Christmas) isn't looking for attention when he buys a homeless man a meal, but grade school teacher Noelle Foster is watching his every move with admiration. His generosity makes him a man after her own heart. While donors give more to children and families in need around the holiday season, Noelle Foster believes in giving year-round after seeing many of her students struggle with hunger and finding a warm bed at night. At a second-chance meeting, sparks fly when Noelle and Nathan share a kindred spirit with their passion to help those less fortunate. Whether they're doing charity work or attending Christmas parties, the couple becomes inseparable. Although Noelle and Nathan exchange gifts, the biggest present is the one from Christ.

One reader says, "A Noelle for Nathan makes you fall in love with love...the love of mankind and the love of God. You cannot read this without having a desire to give and do more, all while being appreciative of what you have."

About *Christmas Greetings*,

Saige Carter loves everything about Christmas: the shopping, the food, the lights, and of course, Christmas wouldn't be complete without family and friends to share in the traditions they've created together. Plus, Saige is extra excited about her line of Christmas greeting cards hitting store shelves, but when she gets devastating news around the holidays, she wonders if she'll ever look at Christmas the same again. Daniel Washington is no Scrooge, but he'd rather skip the holidays altogether than spend them with his estranged family. After one too many arguments around the dinner table one year, Daniel had enough and walked away from the drama. As one year has turned into many, no one seems willing to take the first step toward reconciliation. When Daniel reads one of Saige's greeting cards, he's unsure if the words inside are enough to erase the pain and bring about forgiveness. Once God reveals to them His purpose for their lives, they will have a reason to rejoice. *Come unto me, all ye that labor and are heavy laden, and I will give you rest. Take my yoke upon you, and learn of me; for I am meek and lowly in heart: and ye shall find rest unto your souls.* Matthew 11:28-29

About *A Baby for Christmas,*

Yes, diamonds are a girl's best friend, but unless the jewel is going on Solae Wyatt-Palmer's ring finger, they hold little value to her. When she meets Fire Captain Hershel Kavanaugh, their magnetism is undeniable and there's no doubt that it's love at first sight. Since Solae adores Hershel's two boys from his failed marriage, she wouldn't blink at the chance to become a mother to them. But when it seems as if Hershel doesn't have a proposal on his agenda, she has no choice but to cut her losses and move on. But Christmas is coming. And in order to win Solae back, Hershel must resolve some past issues before convincing her that she possesses everything he wants.

About *A Christian Christmas,*

Christmas will never be the same for Joy Knight if Christian Andersen has his way. Not to be confused with a secret Santa, Christian and his family are busier than Santa's elves making sure the Lord's blessings are distributed to those less fortunate by

Christmas day. Joy is playing the hand that life dealt her, rearing four children in a home that is on the brink of foreclosure. She's not looking for a handout, but when Christian rescues her in the checkout line; her niece thinks Christian is an angel. Joy thinks he's just another man who will eventually leave, disappointing her and the children. Although Christian is a servant of the Lord, he is a flesh and blood man and all he wants for Christmas is Joy Knight. Can time spent with Christian turn Joy's attention from her financial woes to the real meaning of Christmas—and true love? A Christian Christmas is a holiday novella to be enjoyed any time of the year.

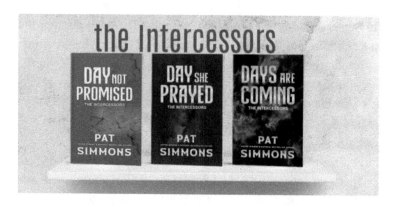

the Intercessors

DAY NOT PROMISED — THE INTERCESSORS — PAT SIMMONS

DAY SHE PRAYED — THE INTERCESSORS — PAT SIMMONS

DAYS ARE COMING — THE INTERCESSORS — PAT SIMMONS

Pat Simmons introduces a new Christian fiction series that reminds readers that the bad guys don't always win, especially when the Lord fights our battles.

In *Day Not Promised*, Omega Addams thought it was a typical workday until a detour on the way home changes everything. She's almost killed, but an innocent bystander, Mitchell Franklin, takes a bullet for Omega during a gas station robbery. In the aftermath, Omega has no idea that God expects her to "pray it forward" until a spiritual battle unfolds before her eyes. Another innocent bystander is in trouble; unless Omega gets her prayer life together, others will die without Christ. It's a chain reaction that highlights the responsibility of a Christian--hot, cold, or lukewarm. It's time to get our acts together. We are our brother's keeper.

In *Day She Prayed*, New Christian convert Tally Gilbert knows the power of prayer and the pain of walking away. She's witnessed family and friends' healing, salvation, and deliverance. There's one holdout, and he's at the top of her prayer list. The love of her life, Randall Addams, won't surrender to the Lord, so Tally ends the relationship. What will it take for Randall to turn to God? Will Tally's prayers be answered, or will Randall—and their love—be lost forever?

Don't underestimate a woman who knows how to pray, has backup, and believes "The Word of God is quick, and powerful, and sharper than any two-edged sword, piercing even to the dividing the soul from the spirit, and of the joints and marrow, and is a discerner of the thoughts and intents of the heart." Hebrews 4:12.

If the devil wants a battle, he picks the wrong woman to fight.

In *Days Are Coming*, the Lord shows my characters how wicked the world has become and how to overcome it.